JANE'S ADVENTURES
IN AND OUT OF THE BOOK

Jane Charrington lives in a huge Cornish castle and
when her parents, the Earl and Countess of Charrington, go to America, the servants are sent on
holiday and Jane is left with Mrs Deal. With
nothing to do one afternoon, Jane goes into a
previously unexplored tower, reputed to be
haunted, and there in an old dusty library she finds
the Book. It is about five feet square and, while
crawling over one of its huge pages, she begins to
sink through it – so begins *Jane's Adventures In and
Out of the Book*.

Jonathan Gathorne-Hardy was born in 1933; his
sister's insatiable demand for stories when she was
much younger led to this book. He has since
written *Jane's Adventures on the Island of Peeg*, as
well as two novels and *The Rise and Fall of the
British Nanny*. At present he is engaged on a third
Jane book: *Jane's Adventures in a Balloon*.

Also by Jonathan Gathorne-Hardy in Piccolo

JANE'S ADVENTURES ON THE ISLAND
OF PEEG

JANE'S ADVENTURES
IN AND OUT
OF THE BOOK

JONATHAN GATHORNE-HARDY

Cover and text illustrations by Nicolas Hill

A Piccolo Book

PAN BOOKS LTD
LONDON

First published in Great Britain 1966 by Alan Ross Ltd.
This shortened edition published 1972 by
Pan Books Ltd, 33 Tothill Street, London, SW1.

ISBN 0 330 23415 3

*Printed in Great Britain by
Cox & Wyman Ltd, London, Reading and Fakenham*

To my sister Rose

CONTENTS

1. THE BOOK

JANE CHARRINGTON stood beside a large cupboard and watched Mrs Deal dashing about the kitchen. She made so many unnecessary journeys that Jane knew one of them would lead to the cupboard. Then Mrs Deal would say,

'Now, don't get in my way. Off you go and play.'

But even this was better than having nothing to do, so Jane stood and watched.

After four minutes Mrs Deal decided she wanted a new duster. Patting the grey bun on the back of her head, she trotted over to the cupboard.

'Boo!' said Jane.

'Good heavens! What a start you gave me!' said Mrs

Deal. 'Now, be a good girl and run along. I've got quite enough to do as it is.

'But I'm so bored,' said Jane. 'What shall I *do*?'

'Now, now, now,' said Mrs Deal, 'I haven't time for larking about,' and opening the door she shoo'ed Jane out.

Mrs Deal was a small thin woman with grey hair tied in a thick, wispy bun. She was always worried and always busy. Jane's father, the thirty-fifth Earl of Charrington, said it gave him a thrombosis just to look at the woman.

But it was in fact really his fault that Mrs Deal had such a lot of work (which, it's true, she enjoyed). Lord Charrington was extremely rich and the very fact of being so rich seemed to keep him busy all the year round. There were frequent trips to London; men would come down with suitcases of papers and cheques for him to sign; and about twice a year he had to go to America. When this happened – as it just had – he always took Lady Charrington with him, and before they went the twenty-five indoor servants, the eighteen gardeners, the six game-keepers and the three chefs would all be sent on holiday. Left behind were Jane and Mrs Deal. Mrs Deal was in charge of everything, and as a reward and because Curl Castle was so large, she was paid the wages of four people during this time (£50 a week).

Because Curl Castle *was* large. It was, in fact, one of the largest in the world. Every owner for hundreds of years had added a new wing or turret or courtyard, and now the castle half filled the Cornish valley in which it stood. Special vacuum cleaners with powerful engines

and seats for the drivers had been built to clean the miles of carpet.

But if Mrs Deal had too much, Jane had far too little to do. She had now been alone in the castle with Mrs Deal for a week and done every possible thing she could think of except one. And that she planned to do after lunch. It concerned a distant tower which was supposed to be haunted. A little girl had gone into it two hundred years before and never been seen since – or not seen alive. But on dark and windy nights her transparent ghost had sometimes been seen walking silently down the dark corridors, with a candle in her hand.

This story had frightened Jane for years, but since it was a warm July day, since she was now twelve, and since she was going nearly mad with boredom, she had at last decided to find out what happened behind the thick oak door which separated the haunted tower from the rest of the castle.

When she had finished lunch she changed into jeans and an old shirt. Then she took a small satchel and put into it a penknife, some chocolate, a torch with an extra battery, two bandages, some Dettol ointment and a handkerchief. Lastly she went to the vacuum cleaner cupboard on the first floor and in a few moments was roaring away down the long, empty, carpet-covered corridors with the satchel bouncing at her waist.

All too soon she reached the door to the haunted tower. She looked at it for some time, her heart beating. It was at the top of six steps, looking very innocent and covered in small brass knobs. After a while, clutching the penknife in her right hand, she very slowly climbed the steps. At the top she stopped again, then putting out one finger she gave the door a tiny push.

To her horror it swung open at once. At first, all she could see was darkness. Too frightened to move, Jane stared into it, expecting at any moment to see the dim figure of the ghost.

Gradually, however, she saw that she was looking up a narrow, winding staircase; and, feeling a little calmer, she took out the torch and began to climb slowly up it.

It was obvious that no one had been there for years. The dust was so thick on each step that she sank into it up to her ankles. Before long she reached the top, and once again was faced by a door covered in brass knobs. But this time it was firmly locked and no amount of shoving would make it open. Half disappointed, half relieved, Jane was about to go back, when her eye was caught by something high above the door, just under the ceiling.

It was a large round hole, and sticking out of the wall all the way up to it were iron bars about a foot apart. At once Jane began to climb up and in a moment she had reached the top, to find that the hole was just big enough for her to squeeze through.

She was in a very high, completely round room. Though the shutters were closed on the windows, one of them had broken open and it was possible to see quite clearly. All round the walls there were very high shelves filled with books, and it was on top of one of these that Jane was now kneeling. Below her she could see a desk, a large globe of the world and, in the middle of the library out of her reach, some tall wooden steps on wheels. However, rolling onto her tummy and sliding her legs over the edge, she managed to climb down.

The dust at the bottom was even thicker than on the stairs, and when she walked it puffed up round her in great clouds, making her sneeze. The first thing she did was to open all the shutters and the windows.

The room, she now saw, though high, was really not very large. Looking around, she noticed that on one of the chairs there was a doll dressed up in curious old-fashioned clothes. But before she could pick it up her eyes were caught by something lying in the middle of the floor. It was a book, and even though it was half covered by dust, Jane could see that it was the largest book she had ever seen in her life.

From top to bottom it measured about five feet and it was at least four feet across. Its cover was of solid black leather half an inch thick, with a title written on it in gold, but in a language Jane couldn't read.

Bending down, she put her fingers under the cover and heaved; though it looked so heavy it opened easily enough, almost as though someone inside had given it a push.

At first there were just seven blank pages, but on the eighth the whole page was taken up by an enormous picture. It was of a square in the middle of a town. The square was full of people all standing and staring at a raised platform. On the platform an old man in a purple cloak was kneeling with his head over a basket. Beside him stood a huge ugly man holding above his head an enormous axe. The picture was drawn in great detail and in bright colours. It looked so real that Jane felt quite frightened.

The same was true of all the other pages. Each consisted of one vast picture, some with a few lines written underneath in the strange language, some without. Turning them over, Jane found one which particularly interested her.

It showed a prison cell, quite bare except for a low wooden bed. High up on another wall a tiny, barred window let a thin stream of sunlight fall onto a table in the middle of the cell. On the table was a half-empty pie-dish, a plate of butter and a full glass of wine. In one corner a young man was crouched by the wall trying, it seemed, to write on it with a fork. Every inch of the picture had been minutely and carefully drawn. Jane could see that on the neck of the young man, below his untidy yellow hair, there was a piece of plaster.

To see more closely exactly what he was doing, Jane crawled on hands and knees to the middle of the picture. As she did so she suddenly saw that about a foot to her left a small piece of paper had been stuck into the edge of the book. She could see that it had something written on it and though the writing was very brown and faded she could just read it:

> *Shut eyes, do not look,*
> *Close your pages on me Book.*
>
> *Turn again, oh Book now turn,*
> *Back through your pages I return.*

I wonder what it means, thought Jane, and almost without thinking she closed her eyes and said aloud in a dreamy voice –

'Shut eyes, do not look,
Close your pages on me Book.'

The moment she had finished the most extraordinary thing happened. The pages of the Book suddenly began to feel soft and fluffy like cotton wool and at the same time the whole picture on which she was sitting turned milky white. The pages grew softer and softer, Jane felt first her feet, then her legs sinking into them, she struggled, reached out to grab the edge of the Book, and then all at once she felt herself slip into a blackness beneath her and go falling, falling, falling.

Someone standing in the library at that moment would have been amazed to see the vast cover of the Book slowly rise up, as though lifted by an invisible hand, and slowly shut itself, apparently squashing the little girl inside completely flat.

2. THE TUNNELLERS

JANE opened her eyes and found that she was standing by the table in the cell she had been looking at a moment before in the Book. She was still holding the piece of paper she had found and, without looking at it again, she folded it up and pushed it into the left-hand pocket of her jeans. A few feet away, with his back to her, the young man was still crouching by the wall. He had not noticed her and she could see that he was chipping with his fork at one of the large stone blocks. He was wearing a loose grey dressing-gown.

After a while Jane coughed and said,

'I say, excuse me.'

The moment she spoke the young man gave a loud

scream, sprang to his feet, and holding the fork in front of him backed nervously away.

'No, no,' he said very quickly and loudly. 'I didn't . . . I promise . . .' But seeing Jane he stopped, looking rather surprised, and then said in a quieter voice.

'Oh, I beg your pardon, I thought you were someone else.' He walked over to the table and picked up the glass of wine. When he had drunk some of it he turned and looked at her.

'That's better,' he said. 'Goodness what a terrible fright. But who are you? How did you get here? Have they put you inside too?' He smiled at her.

'In a way,' said Jane, thinking it would be better to explain about the Book later on.

'I wonder why I didn't hear them bring you in?' went on the young man. 'I suppose I didn't notice. It's true I'm becoming very absent-minded.' He brushed his yellow hair out of his eyes and looked worried for a moment, then said, 'Are you one of us, a Tunneller, I mean?'

'Yes, in a way,' said Jane.

She didn't know what a Tunneller was, but had decided that the young man was so nice that she would like to be with him and his friends whatever they did.

'What were you doing over by the wall?' she asked.

'Trying to escape,' said the young man. 'I thought if I could get that big stone out I might find a tunnel.'

'But it would take you years,' said Jane. 'Look, you've only made a few scratches on it. How long have you been working?'

'A week,' said the young man gloomily. 'I know, I'm hopeless. The trouble is, I was never taught to be an escaper. But I had to do something. They don't let you read here, you know – it's called Ordeal by Boredom. I'm surprised, really, they've put us together.'

'But have you tried any other way?' said Jane. 'Picking the lock or the window?'

'No,' said the young man, 'but it's no good. The window's too small, and you can't pick a lock without hairpins and I haven't any hairpins.'

'What about the bed?' asked Jane.

'The bed?' said the young man.

They looked at it together. It was really just a long wooden box, with a mattress and some grey blankets on it. The young man went over and tried to move it. After some moments puffing and pulling he stood up. 'Screwed to the floor,' he said, staring crossly down at it. Suddenly, however, he dropped to his knees and began to fiddle at its end. 'I wonder . . .' he said, then a moment later, 'Hand me the knife off the table.' After several minutes twisting and poking, he made a pleased noise and with a hard tug pulled off the end. 'There,' he said, holding it up to Jane. '*Not* so hopeless, after all.'

They both knelt and stared into the small black space. 'I can't see a tunnel,' said the young man sadly.

'We can't *see* anything,' said Jane. 'It's far too dark. Look, I think I can just squeeze through. You keep guard.' And before the young man could say anything she began to wriggle under the bed.

'All right,' she heard him say, 'I'll put back the end.' Then, as he did this, his voice became muffled but she thought she heard him say something like 'I'll whistle if there's any danger.'

When Jane had disappeared the young man sat down

at the table and began to finish the pie. He had been doing this for about two minutes when there came a tremendous clattering and banging on the door. It flew open and a huge red-faced man with a beard, a green uniform covered in medals, leather boots up to his knees and with a machine gun dangling from his belt, burst into the cell.

The moment he appeared the young man sprang to his feet, leapt onto the bed and putting his fingers into his mouth gave six or seven piercing whistles.

The red-faced man stopped, his face suddenly becoming redder than ever.

'What the devil are you doing?' he shouted. 'Are you mad? Stand to attention this instant!'

At once the young man stepped off the bed and walked back to the table.

'I'm sorry, Major Wilkinson,' he said. 'I've been in rather a nervous state this morning.'

'Going mad, eh?' said Major Wilkinson. He gave a deep laugh. 'So the Ordeal by Boredom is beginning to work, eh? Well, it doesn't surprise me. Now, is there anything you want, which you can have, and that means it is no good asking for books, paper, ink, musical instruments, cards, soap . . .' He droned on and on, but when he had finished the young man, instead of saying nothing, felt he had to keep the Major talking in case he should hear some strange noise coming from under the bed.

'Well, I wonder,' he said strongly, 'I wonder if I might have some hairpins?'

'Hairpins?' roared Major Wilkinson, once again staring in amazement at the young man. 'You really *have*

gone mad. What the devil do you want hairpins for?'

The young man was always startled when the Major shouted and without thinking he said, 'Why, for the young girl, of course. She needs them for her hair.'

'Hair? Girl?' shouted the Major, looking wildly round the cell. 'What girl? Where?'

'Ah, you wonder where she's gone,' said the young man, beginning to lose his head. 'Quite natural. Well, she slipped under the bed for a few moments to look for her hairpins. That is, not the bed, but out of the door when you came in. I saw her ask one of your men to take her to the matron. So I expect the whole thing will be quite all right,' he went on in a soothing voice. 'The matron will see to the hairpins and we can all relax.'

But the Major was not to be calmed. Instead, with a cruel smile he unhitched his machine gun and advanced upon the young man. 'So you think you need hairpins?' he said. 'You think there's a little girl under the bed, do you? Well, I'll show you, I'll show you!' And before the horrified young man could stop him, he'd raised the machine gun to his shoulder and with a series of deafening explosions fired twenty bullets straight into the bed. Then, laughing loudly and shouting over his shoulder, 'After the Ordeal by Boredom comes the Ordeal by Bullets,' he crashed out of the room.

When Jane had squeezed herself under the bed she had opened her satchel and taken out the torch. At first all she had seen were pieces of fluff and some dead flies. But then, feeling about with her hand, she had found a ring sunk into the floor. It lifted easily, and when she pulled, a small trap-door opened before her. In a moment she had wriggled through.

It was then that she heard above her the shrill whistles of the young man and the thumps as he jumped on the bed. However, she shut the trap-door quickly behind her and set off down the steps leading steeply downwards. On either side were high damp walls, and every now and again sharp corners, as the steps bored deeper and deeper into the castle. Jane followed them for five minutes and then decided she must go back and get the young man. She had just reached the trap-door and was opening it, when she heard the terrible noise of the machine gun and with a zipping noise two bullets shot close past her and went smack, smack, smack down the steps.

Jane got such a fright that she nearly fell backwards, but when nothing else happened she picked up her torch and pulled herself up through the trap-door.

No sooner was she under the bed again, however, than she heard above her the most piteous noise. It was the young man crying. Through his sobs Jane could just hear –

'Oh it's my fault, my fault . . . are you dead? Oh, oh, oh . . . You brute, Wilkinson, brute! brute! brute!'

Jane listened for a while, then she shouted up,

'I'm quite all RIGHT.'

At once the crying stopped and a moment later Jane was clasped in the arms of the young man, who was amazed and delighted to find that she was still alive.

Jane told him what she had seen and, though it was now well on in the afternoon, they decided to escape at once. The young man stuffed a pillow in his bed to make it look as though he were asleep there, and after wrapping up the rest of the pie and putting it in the satchel, they set off.

Jane went first and was soon waiting at the top of the steps. The young man followed and together they started down the steps.

After a little way Jane kicked something which rolled ahead of her like a pebble. Turning her torch downwards she saw a small flat object gleaming up at her.

'Must be one of Major Wilkinson's bullets,' said the young man. 'Why not keep it as a souvenir?'

Jane picked it up and put it in her pocket. After this they walked for a long time. Sometimes steps turned into a tunnel so low that they had to crawl. Sometimes the steps went upwards for a while before continuing down; and several times they must have passed quite close to rooms in the prison because they could hear through the walls the sounds of voices and the tramping of feet, but at last, just as Jane's torch was growing dim, they saw ahead daylight shining through a narrow opening.

The tunnel had ended some way down a mountain. Spread out far below them was an immense valley from which she could see feathery pencils of smoke rising straight into the still, clear air. Down its length curled a distant river shining silver and grey in the early evening light. But she only looked at the view for a moment. Far more interesting was the scene in front of the tunnel.

Immediately before them was a flat open space around whose edge grew a number of small bushes and trees. At a far corner there were parked a number of large cars. In the middle, round three bonfires, sat and strolled a group of perhaps fifty men wearing the same bright green uniform as Major Wilkinson.

'Oh, no,' whispered the young man as they both stared out. 'We're trapped.'

'Who are they?' whispered Jane.

'They must be from the castle,' said the young man. 'Look, do you see those boxes with long wires stretching from them? They are tunnel detectors for finding tunnels underground. We'll be lucky if they don't discover us.'

'What shall we do?' said Jane. The young man said nothing, but continued to stare anxiously out in the fast-fading evening light. At last, putting his mouth close to her ear, he whispered,

'Listen. We have one chance. Do you see those bushes which grow away from us to the left? Well, they reach almost to the line of cars. When it gets a little darker we must try and creep round and then make a run for the nearest car. I only hope I can drive it.'

They waited for ten more minutes and to keep up their strength Jane gave them both some of the chocolate. Then suddenly the young man whispered, 'Now!', and slipped out of the passage mouth and crawled quickly to the first bush.

It was a long and painful journey. Several times Jane felt sure they must be discovered. Once she kicked a stone so that it rolled noisily down a little slope. Once they had to pass so close to one of the sentries that they could hear him softly humming. And once, just as the young man was darting across a small open space between two bushes, one of the sentries cried 'HALT!' in a loud voice and turned round pointing his gun. The young man stopped, and luckily it was now dark enough for the sentry to think him, as he crouched trembling in his dressing-gown, just another bush, because he soon turned round and they saw him light a cigarette. After half an hour of crawling and stooping and running and wriggling they came to the last piece of scrub.

Before them was a wide gap of forty yards, then the cars. They stared in silence until the young man whispered.

'We'll have to chance it. When I say "go" run as fast as you can for the nearest car. Ready?'

'Yes,' whispered Jane.

There was a short pause while the young man looked towards the camp fires, and then all at once he said 'Go'.

They were off. In the darkness Jane seemed to be running very fast. From the right came the noise of the soldiers. Ahead of them the cars grew nearer and nearer. They were more than halfway across when suddenly Jane caught her foot against a large stone and before she could stop herself had fallen flat on her face, letting out a loud yell as she did so.

Immediately a great many things happened at once. There was shouting from the camp. The young man, who had been running in front of her turned round and came running back. And hundreds of powerful torches shone fiercely out of the darkness. There came the sudden sound of guns and almost at once the young man said 'Ow!' very loudly and clutched his left arm. Then he scooped her up with his right arm and she was being carried at great speed towards the car, her ears filled with the rattle and crash of firing guns.

Luckily the door of the nearest car was open. The young man threw her in, then jumped in himself. For a moment they lay there panting. Jane, beginning to recover from the shock, was now suddenly much more frightened. Before, though nervous, she had somehow felt that nothing would happen to her. But now she realized that these men were dangerous. They could, and would if possible, kill her. Kneeling up on the seat she looked anxiously out of the back window.

'Oh, do be quick,' she said. 'They're coming.'

'I'm sorry, it's my arm,' said the young man. However, he pulled himself up and began to push and twist at buttons and switches. Jane stared out, watching the little, running figures with their waving torches come closer and closer. Luckily the car was covered with thick steel plates and had special glass so that the bullets just bounced off.

'Quick,' she said.

'I *am* being quick,' said the young man, feverishly pressing knobs and pulling levers. Jane heard the windscreen wipers begin to swish.

'Damn!' said the young man.

'Quick!' said Jane.

But just as the first soldier was ten yards from the car, the engine gave a sudden roar, the headlights blazed ahead over the valley, and with a jolt it shot forward and in a moment they were careering down the twists and turns of a steep and terrifying mountain road.

Their troubles were still not over. After five minutes the young man said in a weak voice, 'Look, I feel rather faint. Do you think you could steer the car for a while? I'll work the brake with my foot. We don't need to change gears going down hill.'

'I think so,' said Jane. 'I've sometimes sat on my father's knee and steered. I'll try.'

So the young man moved over and Jane slipped into his place. She found it, in fact, quite easy. The steering was specially made so that the lightest touch made it turn, and after a while she began to enjoy spinning the huge car round the steep corners.

Down into the night they sped. The young man didn't faint but sat silently holding his arm, down which Jane could see, in the light from the dashboard, a dark stain was spreading. After a while, however, they began to hear some way behind them the noise of distant hooting and the sound of guns being fired. Quite soon the inside of the car was lit up by the flash of pursuing headlights as the enemy began to gain.

'We'll have to change places again,' said the young man. 'We're not going fast enough.'

They did so, and the car went faster than ever, swaying violently from side to side and going so wildly round the corners that sometimes they skidded within inches of steep precipices. But the pursuit still gained and now on straight bits of road bullets once again went smack against the steel plates.

Suddenly, after turning several sharp corners, there appeared in the headlights a vast tree growing on the left-hand side of the road. Though she saw it only for a moment, its strange shape reminded Jane of a question mark. But when the young man saw it he stopped the car at once.

'Quick, get out!' he said. 'I know where we are.'

They scrambled out, and he leant inside to let off the brake. The car moved slowly forward. Then faster. And faster – until with a rush and a great bounce it disappeared over the edge of the next corner and fell with echoing crashes down the steep cliff. Immediately Jane and the young man turned and stumbled towards the tree, to throw themselves flat in the high bracken which grew around its roots.

They were just in time. In a moment the enemy soldiers came whirling round the corner and went rushing by, shouting and yelling and firing guns into the air.

'Now, let's rest a bit,' said the young man, 'and after that I'm almost certain that quite close to here is the entrance to one of our main tunnels.'

'And first,' said Jane, 'I'll look at your arm.' She gently pulled off his dressing-gown, and turning on her torch (into which she first put the spare battery) she looked at the wound. There was a lot of blood, but as she was not a squeamish girl she wiped it away with her handkerchief and then bound it tightly up with one of the bandages. After this they ate the remains of the pie and finished off Jane's chocolate.

At last, feeling much better, they lay back in the bracken and looked up at the stars. After a while the young man said, 'You know, there is one thing I don't quite understand. I don't think Major Wilkinson knew you had been put into my cell at all.'

'I know,' said Jane. Then, suddenly deciding that she must tell him everything, she said, 'You see, the thing is, I'm not *really* a Tunneller at all.'

'You're not?' said the young man. 'What are you then? Surely not one of *them*?'

'Oh no,' said Jane. 'No, well, you see, it all happened like this.' And then she told him everything; about Lord and Lady Charrington, about how lonely she was in their enormous castle with Mrs Deal, about the haunted part and about the strange book she had found in the old library. He was silent for a while when she had finished, then he said, 'I see. I understand now. You're one of those. I wouldn't have thought so.'

'How do you mean, "one of those"?' said Jane.

'Oh, it doesn't matter,' said the young man. 'You'll find out soon enough. But of course you may not be, in fact I should say you weren't. Even if you are, it doesn't really matter. But I can't tell you. You have to find out from one of them. But perhaps you'd like to know about the Tunnellers?'

'Well, I'd particularly like to know about what you mean by "one of those",' said Jane. 'But if you can't tell me, tell me about the Tunnellers instead.'

'Well,' began the young man. He explained that they were in a country called Kloffus. Some years before, Kloffus had been invaded by its much larger neighbour, Klofron. Many people had been killed and soon the little country had been defeated. However, Kloffus had not given up. After the final battle most of the population had retreated to the gold and silver mines, of which there were a great many, mostly dug deep into the mountains. Since then they had spent their time tunnelling, and now almost the whole of Kloffus, or rather the whole of the underneath of Kloffus, was full of tunnels. When the people of Kloffus felt themselves strong enough they would break out and recapture their country for themselves. The Klofrons, of course, knew that some tunnels existed but they had no idea how many, or where.

'And that's just the trouble,' ended the young man,

'because my job is planning where tunnels should be. When I was captured I had a map of a whole new area of tunnels in the south. It was in code, naturally, but they will soon find out what it means and then we shall have to fill in about forty miles of brand new tunnel and start again.'

'Well, we'd better go back now and try and find the map,' said Jane.

'Yes, but not alone,' said the young man. 'The prison is too well guarded.' He stood up and pulled Jane to her feet. 'I'm almost sure,' he said, 'that near here is a tunnel entrance. Look for a clump of bramble bushes on a little hillock.'

It was very dark now, and as they searched they kept on stumbling. In the end they discovered it among some gorse bushes.

'*Gorse*,' said the young man, as he poked about. 'Of course. I'm afraid the entrance will be very small, but it will only be for a few yards.'

It *was* very small. When he pointed the torch, Jane thought it looked no larger than a big rabbit-hole, but before she could suggest widening it the young man had knelt down, pushed aside some pieces of gorse, and disappeared.

Inside it smelt of earth. She could see nothing and could only just breathe. From ahead came the noise of the young man scrabbling and occasionally a muffled 'ouch' as his bad arm brushed the walls. Suddenly she saw the light of the torch again and almost at once the tunnel widened above and around her. The young man was waiting for her.

'We've joined the main junction tunnel to Mahmelg,

the capital,' he said. 'And that means – yes. Look over there.' He pointed to their right and Jane saw that stretching away into the darkness were several rows of narrow railway lines. On two of these was something like a long steel sausage.

'A tunnel car,' said the young man. 'Come on, climb in.'

There were two seats, one behind the other, covered in soft rubber and very comfortable. The moment they were in, the young man said, 'Ready?'

'Yes,' said Jane.

'Hold tight,' said the young man. There was a loud swooshing noise, and Jane was pressed back into the rubber cushions. As the sausage shot forward a single headlight lit up the tunnel down which they raced.

It was a long journey, but Jane remembered little of it. Now that they were at last safe she suddenly felt very tired. The gentle swooping motion of the tunnel car as it went up and down, the faint hum of its engine, soon lulled her into a deep sleep. She was asleep when the car stopped, she slept through the amazed greetings of the young man's fellow-Tunnellers, and still asleep she was lifted out, and put into a large soft bed in the chambers of the Chief of the Tunnellers himself. She did not even wake when his kind wife undressed her and wrapped her in a shawl.

'We must recapture the plans as quickly as possible.' It was the Chief of the Tunnellers speaking, a large man with a round, kind face and yellow beard. Jane had been woken by his wife, who had brought her breakfast in bed. After Jane had finished it, the woman had said that if she felt rested would she get up and go to the meeting being held to discuss the loss of the plans. When Jane had arrived at the conference room – cut, like all the rooms, out of the solid rock – she had been introduced to the Chief of the Tunnellers, who had shaken her by the hand and said 'Well done, my girl.'

Also in the room were about five other men and her nice young man. He was dressed in a handsome purple uniform like everyone else, but his arm was in a sling and he still looked rather white. He was lying on a low couch and when he saw Jane he gave a grin and waved to her to come and sit beside him.

'Sit beside me,' he whispered. 'I've told them all how brave you were and the Chief wants to give you a medal.'

'As I was saying,' said the Chief, 'the sooner we get the plans the better. How long would it take them to understand our code, Kronin?'

'About two days, sir,' said the young man.

('Kronin,' thought Jane, 'so that's his name. I must remember to tell him mine.')

'We must attack tonight,' said the Chief. 'Now, what method?'

'I suggest, sir,' said one of the other men, 'that we enter by the same tunnel which Kronin escaped from.'

'Excellent idea,' said the Chief. 'Can you remember it, Kronin?'

'Certainly, sir,' said the young man.

'I'm afraid there can be no question of Kronin leading such an expedition tonight,' said a tall, distinguished-looking man sitting on Jane's right. 'His wound is septic and will almost certainly lead to a fever.'

There was a pause, then the Chief said, 'I see, doctor. You're quite sure of that?'

'Of course I can do it,' said Kronin furiously, 'I'm perfectly all right. Look,' and sitting up he waved his wounded arm at the company. But the pain was too great. He turned even whiter, beads of sweat appeared on his forehead, and with a groan he fell back into the cushion in a faint.

'You see?' said the doctor, getting up and moving to his patient. 'The bullet has shattered his bone. I absolutely forbid it.' He felt the young man's forehead, and then, while Jane watched anxiously, signalled to some attendants to carry him out.

'Very well,' said the Chief, 'in that case we will have to think again.' There was a silence while everyone looked at their knees and thought. Then all at once, to her surprise, Jane heard herself saying,

'Excuse me, sir. But I could show you the way. I think I can remember it exactly.'

Everyone looked at her and there came a murmur of admiration. Jane blushed. Then a large smile spread across the Chief's face, 'I believe you could,' he said, 'all right then, now let's discuss plans.'

'There is just one thing,' said Jane timidly.

'Yes, my dear?' said the Chief.

'You don't think that the green men may have found out we escaped and be guarding the tunnel and kill us all when we appear?'

'They may,' said the Chief, 'but it's a risk we'll have to take. The Castle is too strong to attack from outside and we haven't time to dig a new tunnel.'

The rest of the morning was spent in planning the

attack, which was to be guided by Jane. She had been given the rank of Colonel for the occasion.

They set off at eleven o'clock that night. First went the Chief and Jane, followed by one hundred and fifty soldiers in fifteen of the largest tunnel cars. Jane had been given a revolver, which she had strapped round her waist. The tunnel cars travelled at enormous speed, and soon they were all gathered round the tree shaped like a question mark. All the Tunnellers leapt out and began to change the wheels, putting on soft rubber ones so as to make no noise on the road.

The Tunnellers' cars went almost as fast above ground as they had on their lines beneath it, and it did not take long to reach the flat space halfway up the mountain where Jane and the young man Kronin had first seen the enemy. Jane guided them to the tunnel and then the Chief took charge.

'I shall go first,' he said in a quiet voice, 'followed by Colonel Jane. I should like Captain Crispin to bring up the rear.'

Up and up and up. Jane wondered if she could ask the Chief to carry her but decided it was not the kind of thing a Colonel could do. Behind her came the steady tramp, tramp, tramp of three hundred feet. After two hours, Jane and the Chief were standing in the empty cell from which she and Kronin had escaped only the day before. The Chief went and shook the door.

'Too strong to break,' he said, 'call for the Lock Picker.'

'Lock Picker, Lock Picker, Lock Picker!' Before long a fat little man with red hair was pushed panting up through the hole in the bed. He had a large leather bag in his hands in which Jane saw, when she came closer, lots of different sized hairpins. After looking at the lock for a few moments he selected one of these and began twirling it in the keyhole. 'Good man,' said the Chief.

After a few minutes there was a soft click from the door and it swung open. At once Jane and the Chief hurried through and then stood on one side and let the soldiers stream past them. To every third soldier the Chief whispered instructions and then in groups of three they ran off in different directions. In ten minutes the last of the one hundred and fifty had run off into the darkness and then, before she could ask him what she should do, the Chief disappeared too.

Before long the Castle was in confusion. Lights were switched on and switched off. The air filled with shouts and shots and the sound of running feet. And as she hurried along the corridors, Jane would have to jump behind doors to avoid angry groups of men racing past after one another, or fling herself flat on her face as bullets went whizzing above her head. Several times she passed rooms full of green-uniformed men tied tightly hand and foot and gagged with torn pieces of sheet.

She had just passed one of these rooms and was creeping down some steps some way away from the main fighting, when all at once the lights went out again. Jane stood quite still, then very softly began to tiptoe on down the steps. After each step she stopped to listen, but now even the sound of the firing and shouting had died away. One step – stop; one step – stop; one step – stop; she had reached the bottom and was about to feel her way forward, when suddenly an arm shot out of the darkness and she felt herself seized and lifted off the ground. The arm closed round her neck, another gripped her stomach and a deep voice hissed into her ear 'Don't struggle or I'll kill you.' At the same time the lights went on again.

She found herself looking into a huge red face, with a thick red beard. Out of the beard came great hot breaths smelling of onions and wine and rotten meat. 'Well, well, well,' said Major Wilkinson (for it was he). 'Well, if it isn't a little girl. Well if *that's* all we're fighting, an army of little girls, there's nothing to worry about.'

'Put me down, you filthy beast,' said Jane.

Major Wilkinson squeezed her neck and then moving his arm from around her stomach gave her hair a sharp tug. 'Don't you "filthy beast" me, you brat,' he said.

Pulling her hair always made Jane furious. 'Put me down *now*,' she said, 'your breath smells disgusting, re-volting, ough!'

Major Wilkinson's face grew redder than ever and he began to squeeze her so hard that Jane thought he might be going to squeeze her to death. But just then the sound of firing broke out in the distance and at once he tucked her roughly under his arm and set off at a run down the corridor. 'I haven't time to bandy words with you,' he said. 'I'll either have to kill you or lock you up.'

He ran on for some time, with Jane jolting uncomfort-ably up and down on his belt, when all of a sudden he stopped outside a door, pulled a key out of his pocket, unlocked it and threw her in. As she fell through the air she heard him lock the door and shout 'No one will look in here, you brat. I hope you break your legs.'

She must have fallen about twenty feet, but she landed on a large pile of something quite soft and soon she sat up and slid off the pile onto the floor. Then she took her torch out of her satchel.

She was in a high, small room with the door right at the top under the ceiling. She at once saw how lucky she was not to have been badly hurt, because the stone floor was quite bare except for a pile of what looked like sails, made from some red material, neatly heaped in the middle. The room was high for a purpose, because hanging on all the walls were long, thin pieces of wood and hundreds of strings and cords and wires. Nailed to one of the walls was a piece of cardboard with 'LOOK-OUT KITES, LIFTING WEIGHT 5 STONES *ONLY*' printed on it.

Jane did not look round for long. Still furious at having her hair pulled, she dashed up the steps determined to catch Major Wilkinson. The door was locked, but taking out her revolver she put it close to the keyhole, closed her eyes, and pulled the trigger. There was a fearful explosion, the gun jumped violently in her hands, but when she opened her eyes the lock had been completely shot away and the door opened the moment she pushed it.

Once in the corridor she set off at a run to the left, guessing that Major Wilkinson would hardly have gone back the way he had come.

She needn't have hurried. When he had re-locked the door, Major Wilkinson had walked very carefully, stopping every few steps to listen. Jane had run down the corridor and one flight of stairs when she came to a long straight passage. At its far end, creeping close to the wall, she saw the green back and vast green bottom of her enemy.

'Stop!' she said, 'stop, you disgusting, cruel, beastly man!' Then closing her eyes again, and clasping her revolver in both hands she once more pulled the trigger and once more felt the gun leap and crash.

When she opened her eyes a little cloud of smoke was drifting away. Her arms ached. And at the far end of the passage Major Wilkinson lay stretched upon the floor.

At once Jane was filled with horror. 'Oh dear, I've killed him,' she cried; 'oh how awful, how awful.' And throwing the gun away she ran as fast as she could to the motionless figure.

But, in fact, Major Wilkinson was almost all right. When Jane had pulled the trigger the gun had been pointing at the ceiling and the bullet had hit first this, bounced to the floor, bounced back to the ceiling, and had gone on from floor to ceiling, ceiling to floor until finally, moving now hardly any faster than a stone from a catapult, it had bounced off the ceiling onto the top of Major Wilkinson's head and so knocked him out. When Jane reached him a large bruise as big as her fist was swelling from the middle of his head. She had not looked at this for more than a moment when suddenly three Tunnellers appeared round the corner. These promised Jane (whom they respectfully saluted) that they would tie up the Major and take him to the other prisoners.

'How's the battle going?' asked Jane.

'Very well, Colonel,' said one of the men, 'but it takes a little time to winkle the devils out.'

In fact it took until seven o'clock in the morning. By that time the last of the Klofrons had been placed under guard. What was more, the Plan of the Tunnels had been found locked in a box in Major Wilkinson's office. It was clear, from marks on it, that the Klofrons had not yet succeeded in discovering the code.

Now everyone was drawn up on the roof of the Castle. Tired, many of them bruised and battered, they all looked happy in the light of the rising sun.

'Gentlemen,' said the Chief, 'brave soldiers of the Tunnel, I am very proud of you. But before we return underground, I want to single out one of our number for special praise. And that is our new young Colonel here.' So saying, he laid his hand on Jane's shoulder and gently brought her forward. Immediately the air was filled with cries of 'Hear, hear!' and Bravo!' Jane blushed and looked at her feet.

'But for her,' went on the Chief in his embarrassing but kind way, 'our venture could never have succeeded. It was she who boldly guided us to the secret entrance and she who captured, single-handed, the chief officer of this prison, the notorious and evil Major Wilkinson. I have decided to reward such bravery with the highest reward we Tunnellers possess – namely the Order of the Golden Epans. Step forward, Colonel!'

At this speech, renewed cheering broke out and several men lifted Jane upon their shoulders and carried her towards the Chief. He was smiling broadly and holding in his hands the magnificent scrolls and ribbons of the Order of the Golden Epans.

But before he could pin it to her shirt, there came a loud shout and bursting through the door which led back into the Castle, his face white, his arm still in a sling, ran the young man Kronin.

'For God's sake, Chief,' he cried, 'we must fly. All may be lost.'

Immediately an excited murmuring broke out among the men and the three holding Jane put her down. The Chief held up his hand. 'Be quiet,' he cried, then, 'now what's all this about, Kronin? And why are you not in bed?'

'Just after you left,' Kronin said, 'I woke up feeling much better. I stayed in bed till six o'clock this morning and then I took a spare tunnel car and drove it up here. Imagine my surprise when I found, at the entrance to the passage, over two hundred Klofrons gathered round it in the very act of entering. I immediately charged them with my car and managed to scatter them. Then I blocked the hole with my car and hurried up here to warn you.'

At once the Chief began giving orders. 'Good Kronin,' he said, 'you have done well. 'Captain Crispin,' he added, 'take ten men and some gunpowder and go and block the tunnel into the cell before the Klofrons succeed in moving Kronin's car. Sergeant Trindle, double the guard on the prisoners.' The Chief then walked to the edge of the roof, followed by Jane and Kronin and looked over. After a moment she heard him mutter, 'As I feared.'

Looking down, she saw why. Already the bare ground at the foot of the Castle was swarming with hundreds of Klofrons. And every moment more and more of them scrambled up over the steep sides of the mountain.

'We must get help,' said the Chief, 'give me a signalling pistol, someone.' At once a soldier handed him a short pistol with a huge fat barrel big enough to hold a cream bun. Into this the Chief put a large round bullet, which indeed looked rather like a cream bun, pointed it above his head and pulled the trigger. Immediately the bullet shot upwards and burst into a small red cloud high in the air above them. Five times the Chief did this and each time looked anxiously out over the valley. At last he said, 'It's no good. We're too low.'

'What are you doing?' said Jane, unable any longer to control her curiosity.

'Look over there,' said the Chief and pointed across the valley. Jane looked, and saw that he was pointing to the distant mountains which rose beyond it. High as they were in the Castle, the mountains were far higher, and in the early morning sun she could see great stretches of snow glistening on their mighty peaks. 'Among those mountains are our main look-out points,' said the Chief. 'If any of us want help when we are out of our tunnels, we fire one of these red bullets and at once a tunnel is dug to the place where the bullet has been fired from. Unfortunately this Castle is so placed that another mountain is between us and the look-out points. If we were higher it would be all right.'

It was then that Jane had the idea which nearly cost her her life.

'Quick,' she said, 'come with me.' In a few moments she had brought him to the room into which Major Wilkinson had flung her. She opened the door, turned on the lights and pointed excitedly to the notice on the wall. 'There,' she said, 'isn't that the answer?'

The Chief looked at the notice in amazement. 'Goodness me,' he said at last, 'enormous man-lifting kites.'

Then his face fell, 'but they can only carry five stone,' he said, 'and none of us is as light as that.'

'Yes they *are*,' said Jane, her heart beating.

'Who?' asked the Chief, 'I weigh fifteen stone.'

'Me,' said Jane. A gasp of admiration came from Kronin and from the little group which had followed them down from the roof. And the Chief himself seized her by the hand and gave it a hard squeeze, saying, 'Brave girl. It's what I would expect from a winner of the Golden Epans.'

After that all was bustle. Ropes and struts of wood were seized from the walls and huge stretches of the tough red material were unfolded on the floor. Soon the largest kite that Jane had ever seen was standing on the roof. It was fifteen feet high and ten feet across; and in the middle, among the stout wooden struts, was a small chair. 'For me,' thought Jane nervously.

But there was no time to be afraid. The Chief pressed a signal revolver into her hand and three round bullets, explaining how it worked. 'Don't fire it until you see me fire one from down here he said. 'That will mean you are as high as we can get you. And don't worry. These kites are very safe.' Then he suddenly bent forward, picked her up and kissed her. The young man Kronin did the same, and Jane saw tears in his blue eyes. 'Good luck, little girl;' he whispered.

Jane thought 'I haven't told him my name,' and then they were helping her into the seat. She shut her eyes and gripped the arms of the chair.

'One – two – three – NOW!' shouted the Chief, and at *now* ten men bent their backs and with one heave hurled the kite high into the air. For a moment it was motionless, and everyone wondered if it would crash back onto the roof. Then the wind caught it, blew it sharply across to the right, and the next instant it was soaring up into the sky, pulling the rope after it and shuddering a little to the buffets of the air.

Jane kept her eyes tight shut and held her breath. She felt she was going up in the fastest and most unsafe lift in the world. There was a roaring in her ears and her hair was blown in all directions at once. But gradually the upward rush of the kite became slower, the shuddering less violent, and she felt able to look about her.

The view was terrifying but wonderful. Away to her right rose peak after peak of the distant mountains; to her left was a vast plain with a tiny blue line at its end which must have been the sea; and below her feet, no bigger now than a teacup, was the Castle, with the thick black rope rising from its roof. This rope was quite tight and Jane could hear a deep humming as it vibrated in the wind. As she looked down a large white bird flew between her and the ground, brushing the rope with its wing tips.

Just after it had passed, there came a tiny puff of smoke from the Castle and a small red cloud appeared about sixty feet below her. Immediately, Jane took the signal pistol in both hands, pointed it up through the top of the kite and pulled the trigger. Far above her a little red cloud blossomed in the sky. But when she looked across the valley to the mountains there came no answering signal. Nor was there any after the second. And when the third red cloud had been blown away and there was still no sign, she was about to drop the pistol in despair, when all at once, from the top of one of the distant, though not the highest peaks, there rose a slender column of green smoke. The signal! And they had seen it from the Castle. Looking down, Jane could just see tiny figures jumping about and running around the roof with excitement.

It was at this moment that disaster struck the kite. The Klofron soldiers had watched its rise into the sky with amazement. 'Surely,' they thought, 'no one expects to escape by kite.' But when the little red signal clouds began to puff above it they guessed that the Tunnellers were calling for help and at once began to fire their rifles and revolvers, hoping to bring it down or kill the person in it. The kite was far too high for any of their bullets to reach it, but just as the Chief was ordering it to be pulled in again, a stray bullet hit the rope and with a twang cut clean through it.

At once the kite gave a fearful lurch and started to plunge downwards. There came a groan of horror from the watchers on the Castle and a cheer of triumph from the Klofrons. Jane was flung forward and only saved herself by dropping the pistol and clinging with both hands to the wooden seat.

But the wind so high in the sky was very strong indeed and the rope still dangling from the bottom of the kite was very heavy. After falling for a few seconds, the kite was suddenly seized by an extra powerful blast of wind and in a moment was soaring up into the air again, carried in its gusty arms. The Castle was so far below that she could hardly see it. A little group of white clouds appeared on her left and then seemed to float downwards as she sped up past them. Now she was level with the tops of the highest mountains, now rising above them. 'Perhaps I'll be blown to the moon,' thought Jane, beginning to enjoy herself even though she felt frightened, 'or Mars.'

But the higher it rose, the stronger blew the wind. It deafened Jane with its roaring and made it difficult to breathe. And as she watched, one of the smaller struts broke with a snap and was instantly whirled away. And then another, and another, and then the wind caught a strip of red material and tore it off with a great ripping noise. And suddenly, with a loud cracking of wood and a flapping of stuff, the whole kite was torn into shreds as though by a giant claw, and Jane was flung out into the air and began, with terrifying speed, to fall back towards the earth, turning over and over, head over heels, down through miles of empty sky.

'I shall be smashed to pieces,' she thought, as a cloud rushed past; 'I shall bounce and bounce and bounce,' as she shot down level with the tops of the mountains. 'Perhaps I'll land in a deep river,' she said as a startled bird flew out of her way.

And then, as the ground came racing up to her, as she saw now trees now clouds in her spinning fall, she suddenly remembered the piece of paper she had found in the Book so long before and had stuffed into the pocket of her jeans. In a moment she had pulled it out, in a moment opened it and held it to her face, and just before she hit the ground, when she could actually see the rocks and stones and little bushes of the hillside rushing towards her, she cried at the top of her voice:

'TURN AGAIN, OH BOOK NOW TURN,
 BACK THROUGH YOUR PAGES I RETURN.'

Her fall was checked. The air around her turned milky and felt more and more like cotton wool. And she started to rise upwards almost as fast as she had just been falling. She was saved.

3. THE FLOOD

AT ONCE Jane guessed what had happened. And when she sat up she found, as she had expected, that she was sitting on the open Book in the old library. It was night, but there was enough light from the moon for her to see the high bookshelves, the desk and the library steps. She could also just see, when she looked down between her knees, that the picture of Kronin in his cell was no longer there. The page on which she sat was completely blank.

It did not take her long to climb out of the library, and hurry back to the vacuum cleaner. She pressed the starting button, turned on the headlights specially put in by Lord Charrington so that Mrs Deal could do the carpets at night and was soon whirring down the mile-long corridor. She had almost reached the end, when all at once she saw in the headlights an enormous pool of water. Before she could brake, the cleaner raced into the middle, sending great waves whooshing up the wall on either side, and came to a spluttering stop.

For some moments Jane sat doing nothing, amazed. It was completely dark, because the lights of the cleaner had gone out when the engine stopped. In the silence she could now hear the gulping and swirling of water as though the Castle were slowly sinking into a lake. What could have happened? Perhaps Mrs Deal had left all the baths on by mistake. 'MRS DEAL,' she shouted, 'MRS DEAL, WHERE ARE YOU?' But there was no answer.

'I shall have to wade,' thought Jane. She took off one shoe and sock and dipped her toe in. Luckily the water was only a few inches deep, so she took off the other shoe and sock, rolled up her jeans and, shining the torch ahead, set off. Under the water the carpet felt cold and furry, like stiff moss.

Quite soon she came to the place where all the corridors on the first floor joined a large landing running round the front hall. It was light here from the moon, so Jane turned off her torch and moved over to the balcony, hoping to feel her way to the main stairs.

But at the balcony she saw the most extraordinary sight. Instead of stopping at the edge, the water on the landing continued straight on. The entire hall was filled with water. That meant, thought Jane, that the kitchens must be flooded, and the drawing-rooms, dining-rooms, sitting-rooms, cellars, even, perhaps, the gardens, the whole valley. And as her eyes grew accustomed to the moonlight she could see floating on the water a fleet of familiar objects: Lord Charrington's wooden shoe-trees, a sofa, lamps, chests, tennis rackets, a tea cup, tables and, suddenly, Mrs Deal's Wellington boots.

At the sight of the boots Jane began to feel frightened. What had happened? Where was Mrs Deal? Was she drowned? And then, tired, alone, cold, wet, hungry, Jane began to cry. 'Mrs Deal,' she sobbed, 'Mummy, Daddy, where are you? What shall I do? Help me, help me, help.' But again there came no answer except the gentle swish of the dark water and the bumping sound as bits of floating furniture knocked together in the hall.

It was at this moment that a door opened just behind her and a bright light shone out. At the same time a well-known voice said, 'Is that you, Lady Jane? Goodness me, whatever have you been doing? I found a vacuum cleaner missing and you know your father doesn't allow jaunts on the cleaners.'

'Mrs Deal!' cried Jane. 'Oh darling Mrs Deal,' and splashing across the carpet she flung herself into Mrs Deal's arms. 'Oh Mrs Deal, I saw your gumboots and I thought you'd been drowned.'

'There, there,' said Mrs Deal, 'there, there, you know quite well I'd never let myself be drowned, you silly gumption.' But encumbered though she was by a hissing hurricane lamp, she swung her arms round Jane and lifted the little girl up to give her a dry, gentle kiss. 'Stop your crying,' she said, 'all's well that ends well. And now up you come to the nursery floor. The water is still rising and we'd best get you some supper.'

When they reached the nursery, Mrs Deal pulled off Lord Charrington's duck-shooting waders which she was wearing and, while she dried Jane in front of the fire, explained what had happened.

Apparently the little dam at Combe Reservoir had broken on Wednesday night and the waters had at once rushed into Curl Valley and flooded it. Luckily it was only the small reservoir and the Authorities said the water would go down in a few days. 'They offered to take me off,' said Mrs Deal, 'but I refused. I've telegrammed your father and asked for instructions. Now you, my girl, must have something to eat and then off to bed.'

Jane had some bacon and eggs and then Mrs Deal gave her a wash and tucked her up. However, before Mrs Deal blew out the candle, they had one small argument. She was folding up Jane's jeans when a small, flat object dropped to the floor.

'What's this,' said Mrs Deal, picking it up.

'A bullet,' said Jane.

'Nonsense,' said Mrs Deal, 'a bullet in Curl Castle indeed.'

'It's my bullet,' said Jane, 'and please give it to me.'

'Certainly you may have it,' said Mrs Deal, 'but a bullet it is not.' She looked at it a moment and then, smiling down in a kindly grown-up way, gave it back. 'I would say it was dentist's filling from a particularly large tooth,' she said; 'probably from your grandmother, old Lady Dorothy Charrington, who was famous for the size of her teeth. Yes,' she finished, 'that's what it is. A large filling from one of the largest of old Lady Charrington's lovely back teeth.' And bending down Mrs Deal kissed Jane softly and dryly goodnight.

*   *   *

In the morning they had a breakfast of baked beans and eggs, and tea with condensed milk. Mrs Deal had managed to move nearly all the food from the store room into the nursery before the ground floor was flooded and now about four hundred tins were neatly piled there. There were also some bottles of wine which, Mrs Deal explained, they might need for medicinal purposes. Mrs Deal had also rescued a primus stove and plenty of paraffin.

When Jane looked out of the nursery windows, the hot sun was shining onto the gleaming water which stretched all round them to the curvy hills of the little valley. Everywhere, most of their trunks out of sight under the water, the tops of the trees stuck up like vast floating bushes. She could see the ropes of her swing, which was hung from a high branch of a cedar on the lawn, suddenly disappearing under the surface and when she looked down at the drive underneath the window she could see the dim wavery black outline of a car standing at the front door, completely covered by water.

During breakfast they discussed plans.

'The water has been rising,' said Mrs Deal. 'I don't know what we should do, I'm sure. Still no word from your father.'

'We must rescue things,' said Jane. 'First precious things like pictures and all the tables and then things like blankets and food and nails and gunpowder. No,' she went on, 'perhaps the gunpowder and the nails and things first. We may be here for weeks or months or even years. Have we any weapons for killing food, etc?'

'Weapons my foot,' said Mrs Deal briskly. 'Luckily

the telephone is still working and I rang the Post Office this morning. They said the water should be going down by this evening. You've got too much imagination, my girl. But some of the nice Chippendale we *ought* to carry out of harm's way, and all the pictures.'

Jane's first move was to the summer room, where were stored all the games and fishing nets and flippers she played with in the summer. Here she found two Li-Lo's and a rubber dinghy. She blew them all up, tied them together, and then started up the corridor, towing behind her a bobbing convoy whose rubber colours were bright in the morning sun.

She would tie her fleet outside a room, wade in and carry out whatever seemed valuable and pile it onto the Li-Lo's and into the dinghy. Then she would slowly drag the whole load back and heap it at the bottom of the nursery stairs so that Mrs Deal could help her drag it up.

After a quick lunch of potted shrimps, ham, mashed potatoes and tinned peaches and condensed milk, they continued their work.

Jane, however, soon grew tired of collecting furniture and pictures. Not only was it very hard work, but also there was so much left in the myriad rooms, galleries and cupboards and bathrooms of the first floor that it seemed quite pointless to continue. Without telling Mrs Deal, therefore – who was in any case far out of sight and sound in the distant East Wings of the Castle – she set out to gather more practical objects.

First she went to Lord Charrington's gun room and loaded a Li-Lo with cartridges and guns. Having stored these in her nursery cupboard she went to the Forestry room. Here her father stored the ropes, axes, choppers, cutters, nails, etc, which were needed for all the work on the estate. Nearly all of these Jane took and locked in her toy cupboard, which was very large. She also took eighteen large, sealed tins of best quality gunpowder. This her father used for blowing tree stumps out of the ground. The tins were very heavy and only three could be safely loaded into the rubber dinghy at a time. And from her father's study she collected three bottles of gin and put them in the toy cupboard. Mrs Deal's plan of medicinal wine was sensible, but Jane felt that for a real emergency spirits might be needed.

And all the time the water rose. Inch by inch it climbed until the bottom, then the second, then the third of the wide nursery stairs were covered. It loosened the wallpaper from the walls so that it floated out in a broad frieze, like curiously coloured seaweed. First it came to Jane's knees, then her thighs and finally her last trips had to be made sitting in the dinghy, pushing aside, as she went, the chairs and tables which had floated out of the rooms and were making aimless, slowly twirling journeys by themselves down the flooded corridors.

It was late evening when Jane decided that she had done enough. She made a last visit to the Forestry room and loaded up with some more gunpowder and a large box of wind-and-rain-proof matches. From everywhere came the sound of gently bumping furniture as sluggish currents moved it about, a steady dripping and running and sucking noise, and all along the walls and ceilings there was the flickering reflection of the evening sun off the water.

Jane steered round a waterlogged sofa, and turned the

corner into the last bit of corridor before the nursery stairs. As she did so she heard Mrs Deal calling:

'Lady Jane? Lady Jane? I need help. Please come and help me. Lady Ja-a-a-a-nne.'

'Coming, Mrs Deal,' shouted Jane, and began to paddle the heavily weighted dinghy as hard as she could. 'Coming.'

As she came out of the corridor onto the landing round the main hall she saw the most odd sight. Across the other side of the hallway, and a quarter way up the nursery stairs, Mrs Deal had propped herself against the banisters. Above her, and held in place by her thin, straining shoulders, was a vast grand piano. By some miracle of wedging and shoving she had managed to push it well clear of the water. Now, defeated by its immense weight, she could go no further, and was only just able to keep it in place.

Jane paddled towards her. 'What are you doing, Mrs Deal?' she called. 'We'll never get that up the stairs. Let it slide back.'

'We can't,' panted Mrs Deal, 'your mother's favourite Steinway. Ruin the keys. Just get it a little higher then we can tie it out of harm's way.'

'But it's huge,' said Jane.

'It's slipping,' said Mrs Deal suddenly, in a weak voice.

'I'm coming,' said Jane, paddling as hard as she could. 'Hold on.'

But she was too late. Even as she watched, the piano, with a tiny twang from its strings, began to move. 'Oh dear,' panted Mrs Deal, forced down a step. 'Twang' went the piano. 'Oh dear,' cried Mrs Deal. And then,

before Jane's horrified eyes, the piano began to bump noisily down the stairs, faster and faster, its strings jingling and jangling and tingling, sweeping Mrs Deal irresistibly before it, until with a final ringing of dis-organized chords it surged into the water and floated swiftly out into the middle of the hall, where it spun slowly round and round, bobbing gently. Of Mrs Deal, there was no sign.

'Mrs Deal, Mrs Deal,' cried Jane. 'Where are you?'

She need not have worried. When the piano swept into the water and through the balcony, Mrs Deal was carried with it, clinging to the keyboard. Once in deeper waters, she let go and at once sank to the bottom, dragged down by the weight of Lord Charrington's rubber waders. Now, peering down into the still clear depths, Jane saw her shake these off and in a few mo-ments rise to the surface not far from the piano and swim energetically to the gap in the balcony.

'Are you all right, Mrs Deal?' said Jane, paddling up to her. 'I thought you'd gone to a watery grave.'

'Nonsense,' said Mrs Deal, 'ever since a girl I've been a good swimmer. What a lot of trouble this water's giving us – and the mess!' As she spoke, she twisted the long tresses of grey hair that hung round her shoulders from her undone bun. 'Now up we go,' she said, 'it's dry clothes for me and a good hot supper and bed for you.'

Jane waited until Mrs Deal was changing her clothes, then hurried down to carry up the rest of the gun-powder and hide it in her toy cupboard. She also dragged the dinghy up and left it outside the nursery door, just in case.

They were both tired, and after a dinner of chicken, tinned peas, and condensed milk, they went to bed. Though it was not enough of an emergency to reveal the gin, Jane suggested Mrs Deal have some glasses of medicinal wine. This she did.

As she fell asleep, Jane found herself wondering if she would ever have another adventure in the Book. She decided that, if the waters went on rising, she would go to the tower next day and just make sure it was, as she thought, really one of the highest in the Castle and so quite safe.

She was woken at six o'clock by the early morning sun shining onto her face. She lay sleepily for a while, and then all at once decided it would be more fun to get up and go for a quiet paddle in the dinghy before Mrs Deal was awake.

At once she sat up, put on her dressing-gown, swung her legs over the bed and – *felt water*. Water! An inch deep all over the nursery floor, water gently creeping higher and higher through the night, filling the house, burying them – water! Jane seized her boots and splashed over to the door. Once more she saw a flooded corridor, the round rubber dinghy floating some way down it. She hurried back and opened the window. It was true. The water had silently risen a whole storey during the night; in the distance, only the very tops of the trees now waved above the surface.

At once, all was bustle. She woke up Mrs Deal who, without even waiting to take her hair out of curlers, rose magnificently to the occasion. 'First we must have breakfast,' she said, 'then carry as much as we can up to the roof. There's no telling where this will end.' Jane agreed.

They both dressed; had a quick breakfast of boiled eggs and tea; and then started to carry essential provisions up to the roof.

It was after the second of these journeys, when they were in the nursery loading their arms with tins and blankets, that the sudden chugg-chugg-chugg of an engine made them both hurry to the window.

Out in front of the Castle, steering between the tussocks, which was all that remained of the tall trees on either side of the main gates, a small motor boat was speeding towards them.

'Ahoy!' shouted Jane. 'Ah-o-o-o-y, ahoy!' The young man who was driving swung his motor boat round and stopped just under the nursery window.

'Good morning,' said Jane, 'what's happened?'

'Cracks has appeared in the big dam at Combe,' said the young man, 'been a lot of big leaks. But they say she'll hold. I've been sent to take you off of here. And I've a telegram for Mrs Deal.'

'Oh dear, where are my spectacles?' said Mrs Deal, fussing in her apron pockets. 'That will be your father. Now give me the telegram, young man.' He rocked his boat close to them and handed over the yellow envelope. Mrs Deal tore it open and together they read:

'Stand fast. Report position. Full instructions following. Charrington.'

'Well, that's that,' said Mrs Deal. 'I'm afraid we can't

come with you, young man. There's far too much to do here, as his Lordship knows.'

'But I've particular orders,' said the young man in a worried voice; 'I was told "rescue all inmates of the Castle".'

'Only people who are in trouble need rescuing,' said Jane, 'and we are not in trouble. We will stay in the Gazebo on the roof till the waters go down. And my father quite agrees.'

'I only take instructions from Lord Charrington,' said Mrs Deal; 'or Lady Charrington,' she added.

'Or me,' said Jane.

'Now then, my girl,' said Mrs Deal.

'Well I don't know,' said the young man, 'I've had me orders. But they say the dam will hold. I think I'll go back and if it looks any worse come straight back. Well cheerio. Mind you stay on the roof.' And with a wave of his hand, he turned the motor boat and went roaring straight as an arrow over the fountain, between the topmost leaves of the gate trees and was soon gone.

They had little time to worry about his departure. The noise of the cracking of the big dam spurred them on, and soon the pile of tins and blankets, beds and bottles began to fill the eight-sided Gazebo on the roof.

By twelve o'clock they had carried up almost more than the Gazebo could hold.

'Now you run along and play awhile,' said Mrs Deal at last, 'and I'll get this lot sorted out. No sliding on the slates, mind. We don't want the rain getting in.'

Jane, however, had other plans. She hurried down the stairs again and went straight to the toy cupboard. The water on the nursery floor had now risen above her knees, but she had been careful to put the tins of gunpowder, the wind-proof matches and the gin on a top shelf.

It took twelve journeys to carry them up and hide them in a small wooden shed where the Castle chimney-sweep kept his brushes and rods. It was well out of sight of the Gazebo, but Mrs Deal had already begun dusting and Jane could have driven an elephant across the roof without her noticing it.

When she had carried everything up, she went down one last time to get the dinghy. It had floated all the way down the corridor and was now gently bobbing about at the far end. Jane squelched up to it over the spongy carpet, swung it round and was about to return, when all at once she heard a distant rumble; at the same time the water in the corridor surged up her legs and then fell back, as though the Castle had been tilted. Nervously she looked back over her shoulder out of the window. And there she saw a sight so frightening that, as she afterwards said, terror turned her knees to jelly.

Not half a mile away, where Curl Valley opened out into the wider Inkpen valley, a great grey cliff, seeming hundreds of feet high, its mile-long top sparkling and breaking in the sun, was racing towards the Castle. And as it came, hurtling ever faster, its rumbling grew to a roar, its roar to the rocky bellows of the most terrible earthquake, and the walls and ceilings and floating furniture and Jane herself began to jump and tremble as though with huge million-ton feet a giant were charging up to crush them into pieces.

The big dam had burst at Combe. As Jane had come

down the stairs, a great crack had suddenly leapt from its bottom and shot two hundred feet to its top. As Jane had squelched up the corridor, the main reservoir had begun to burst through and workmen had fled for their lives. And as she had turned to take the dinghy back, the whole dam had crashed to the ground, a mountain of grey, turbulent, angry water had sprung forth and swept irresistibly into Curl Valley.

She just had time to fling herself into the dinghy and take a tight hold of the side ropes, and then the huge wave dashed against the Castle.

The walls stood firm – all except the North Wing, which was instantly washed away. But the windows did not. There was a moment's pause, an inky blackness while the waters whirled outside, and then with a crash a thousand casements broke and the deluge poured in.

The first terrible wave knocked Jane unconscious for a minute. The dinghy was engulfed and pressed down under the weight of water. But in a moment it had bobbed to the top and Jane found herself racing down the corridor on the surface of a deafening river. But it was a river that was rising. From all sides other rivers spouted from the doors of all the rooms, and soon, bouncing off the walls and spinning in the eddies, Jane was speeding along just below the ceiling.

Just before she was crushed against the top, the corridor ended in a short staircase to the floor above. In a flash the dinghy was lifted up it by the surge of water, and then went hurtling down another corridor, bounding round corners, whirling past pictures, which were buried even before she had passed them, and soon was once again just below the ceiling. Jane had to crouch low to avoid the chandeliers, soon she could touch the ceiling, then was forced to lie flat and holding her breath, heard the sound of the dinghy scraping the ceiling as it was driven higher, and felt a cold rush as water was forced over the sides; and then, just as she was expecting to be drowned, there was a loud crash and the dinghy shot forward into darkness and began to rise rapidly upwards.

What had happened was quite simple. The combined weight of water, Jane, branches and furniture had been too much for a thin wall at the end of the corridor on the third floor. It blocked the corridor off from an old staircase which led up to the roof, and when it had broken let Jane and the dinghy shoot through. As the old staircase filled with water, so up rose Jane, carried safely on its surface.

Carried safely, and carried ever more slowly. Because now the worst was over. The waters from the broken dam, sweeping past the Castle to fill the whole valley, had begun to find their proper level, and by luck this was just below the level of the roof. After five minutes Jane found that she had stopped rising and as her eyes grew accustomed to the darkness she saw before her a small door, secured by a simple bolt. She opened it and sunlight streamed in. Before her was the roof, and in a moment she had stepped out onto it and pulled the dinghy out behind her.

4. THE EXPLOSION

THE view from the roof was desolate and strange. On all sides the sunlit waters stretched to the enclosing hills, but now no tree top, no gatepost, chimney or wall poked above their ruffled surface. Only the roof of the Castle, like a vast, strange raft floating on a grey sea, gave comfort to the little girl. The tower which held the old library with the Book rose highest above the surrounding flood. And when Jane walked to the balustrade, she saw that the water whirling only a foot or two below the gutters was black and dirty, thick with branches, pieces of gate and fence, and other more horrid things.

The entrance to the staircase which had so

miraculously saved her life was not far from the Gazebo.
As she drew close to it, she shouted 'Mrs Deal, Mrs
Deal – I'm all right,' and began to look forward to tell-
ing about her adventures.

But Mrs Deal had worked herself into a positive
frenzy of dusting and cleaning and mopping up, and was
far too busy to take any notice. In its first rush the wave,
only about sixty feet high despite its terrifying appearance, had swept into the Gazebo. Mrs Deal was
now busily mopping it out and at the same time cooking
lunch on the primus stove. She had also, Jane was surprised to see, put on several large jerseys, gloves, an
overcoat and wrapped three dusters round her neck,
even though the sun was shining as hotly as ever outside.

'I've had a *terrible* adventure,' cried Jane, bursting
excitedly into the Gazebo.

'I'm sure you have, dear,' said Mrs Deal, speaking
calmly and not for a moment stopping her mopping and
dusting, 'and I've caught a terrible cold. Now get those
wet clothes off, there's enough water about without you
adding to it; we must get something warm inside us as
soon as this broth has cooked.'

Though Jane felt disappointed at not being able to tell
her story, she knew better than to try and talk to Mrs
Deal in a dusting mood.

During lunch Mrs Deal's cold grew rapidly and
visibly worse. She sneezed a great deal, blew her nose,
and began to talk in a thick, hoarse voice. This sudden
collapse did not worry Jane. Mrs Deal often 'went
down' with something, and soon recovered.

After lunch, however, when Mrs Deal gave five

enormous sneezes all in a row, she thought it would be kind to give her some gin. She therefore fetched a bottle from the chimney-sweep's shed and filled a tumbler with the watery liquid. 'Here, Mrs Deal,' she said, 'I think in this emergency you should have some spirits. My father always says they are very good for a cold.' Mrs Deal took the glass gratefully.

'Dank you, my dear,' she said in her new, hoarse voice, 'dat 'ould be very kind.' And spluttering a little, and pausing twice to sneeze and blow her reddening nose, she soon finished it.

'More?' asked Jane.

'No dank 'oo,' said Mrs Deal, coughing, 'dad will do. I'll have some bore ad dea-dime.'

'But what shall we do *now*?' said Jane.

'We mud wait till we are rethcued,' said Mrs Deal mournfully, 'there's nudding for it.'

'But what will my father say?' said Jane. 'Oughtn't we to stick to our post till the water goes down? Why, I think it's a little lower already.'

'Nudding for it,' repeated Mrs Deal, her voice getting slower, 'if we had a plug we could pull it out. But the water will day and day and we can't do nudding. Furniture ruined. We mud wait dill they come wid a boat – and a thtretther,' she added, so low that Jane could hardly hear her.

But she wasn't in any case listening. Because when Mrs Deal said 'Plug,' the most wonderful, brilliant, exciting plan had sprung into her head. 'Plug.' *That* was the answer – *pull out the plug*!

Of course, she couldn't tell Mrs Deal. Even ordinarily she would have been most unlikely to agree to Jane's simple but dangerous plan. Now, weakened by her cold, dizzy with gin, she certainly wouldn't. Luckily, however, Mrs Deal had fallen asleep. It was the work of a moment to cover her warmly up with some blankets, and slip outside.

Once there, she became very busy. First she carried the dinghy over to the balustrade, lifted it onto the water, and tied it firmly to the edge. Next she hurried to the chimney-sweep's shed and one by one carried three tins of gunpowder and lowered them gently into the dinghy. Then she put the wind-and-rain-proof matches in her pocket and wrote a short note to Mrs Deal.

'Do not worry. I have gone to blow up mushroom tunnel. Back in time for tea or supper. Don't fuss.

Love, Jane.'

Then she climbed over the balustrade, settled herself in the dinghy and cast off. At once the currents which were still moving in the flood waters caught hold of the dinghy and in a moment it was moving rapidly away from the Castle.

Jane's idea was this. Many years before, her father's great-grandfather, the thirty-second Lord Charrington, had decided to grow mushrooms in Curl Valley and sell them in France. To make this easier he had dug a long tunnel beneath the hills at the end of the valley so that it should join with the sea at the other side. Unfortunately he had died before his scheme could be tried, and the tunnel, because it used to become filled with salt water at high tides, had been blocked up with bricks at the end nearest the sea. It must now, Jane realized, be full of flood water, and if she could blow up the bricks at the sea end then the water would pour out. Just, as Mrs Deal had said, like pulling a plug out of a bath.

But she could already see that it was going to be harder than she had thought. Luckily the currents seemed to be sweeping her towards the far end of the valley. But even then, though she paddled as hard as she could, and though the long rim of Curl Castle roof soon grew small behind her, the distant hills seemed to be no nearer. Jane was strong for her age, but gradually she grew more and more tired. The dinghy began to move slower and slower. The wide grey waters stretched all round her, and, though she knew it was foolish, she suddenly began to imagine strange monsters moving in the trees and fields buried underneath.

Just when she was about to give up in despair, a light breeze sprang up. Soon it freshened to a wind and before long the dinghy was being blown merrily over the small waves with Jane resting against its rubber sides.

Even so, it was four-thirty before, with a gentle thump, she reached the shore. She climbed out, tied the dinghy to a nearby bush, and unloaded the gunpowder.

It took her two hours to carry the three heavy tins, one at a time, to the top of the valley. Two hours which left her boiling hot and exhausted. But reach it she eventually did. Suddenly the hill fell away in front of her and at its foot was the peaceful, sparkling sea. After a while Jane sat up and turned to look down at the valley behind her. This, too, looked peaceful in the slanting rays of the sinking sun. From side to side, from end to end, the waters of Combe Reservoir filled it, making a

vast, almost circular lake. Birds glided in the air above it
and some landed on it. And these waters had already
begun to clear. She could see an oblong, dark patch
where the branches of Currel Wood must have been
waving in the slow currents; a light patch where the
cornfield was; and a wavery, pale ribbon which was the
road to Inkpen winding away under the water. Only in
the middle, like a huge, irregular tray covered in chim-
neys, turrets, towers and roofs, the top of the Castle
broke the surface.

The downward journey was very much easier and
faster than the journey up. Jane reached the bottom in
an hour. At half past seven, she was standing before the
bricked-up entrance to the tunnel.

The mushroom tunnel was nine feet high and ten feet
wide, and the bricks blocking it had been built five feet
thick to withstand the batterings of the winter storms.
But in the very middle at the bottom, where some bricks
had crumbled away, the sea had scooped out a small,
smooth cave, about two feet deep.

Into this Jane pushed her way, shoving the tins of
gunpowder one by one in front of her. She lay two of
them side by side, and then opened the third tin and, as
she had often seen her father do, poured a large mound
of black gunpowder grains in between them. Next she
crawled backwards pulling the open tin with her, so that
a black trail led from the tins inside the wall out onto the
beach. Once there, Jane lifted up the open tin and, holding it between her knees, walked slowly backwards letting the gunpowder trickle out in a wavy black line.

After she had gone some way down the beach, she
turned up the hill again. There was no knowing what

might not happen when the explosion came and she would be safest if she went quite high up.

At last she felt she had gone high enough. She dropped an extra dollop of gunpowder on the ground, and then slowly went back, putting down more gunpowder wherever the black trail looked thin. It was a quarter past eight when she finally reached the blocked-up tunnel again.

She crawled in and put the last tin beside the two others. Then she covered them quickly with some rocks that were lying around. For some reason she was beginning to feel rather nervous; the sound of the sea seemed somehow frightening behind her, and when she stopped to listen she thought she could hear the noise of the flood waters moving in the black tunnel behind the wall.

Without waiting to pile more stones, Jane backed out of the hole and ran as fast as she could along the beach and back to where the trail of gunpowder ended. There she sat down, panting, and pulled the wind-and-rain-proof matches out of her pocket.

Below her, the sea lapped on the shingle, its silvery surface ruffled by a gentle wind. The hillside rose above her, very black and very still.

'Wow!' thought Jane.

But she did nothing. What would happen when the gunpowder exploded? Perhaps the whole hill would collapse. Her father had always said it was dangerous. She would be buried in an avalanche.

Very quickly, as though getting into the sea on a cold day, Jane lit a match and touched the little pile of gunpowder at her feet.

At once, with a fizz, it was off. A bright but small flame went running down the hill. Some times it went out of sight and Jane thought it had gone out. Then it appeared again farther down. Now it had reached the beach, now was running along the shingle, now turning up towards the tunnel. And then, craning round the boulder behind which she was crouching, she saw the flame disappear inside the hole. There was a pause, a silence, and then suddenly a bright, shooting flash of orange light and the most tremendous, rocking, crashing EXPLOSION Jane had ever heard. It shook the ground and threw her flat on her back. And behind it, even as she fell, she heard a deep, rumbling, terrifying roar.

When Jane stood up again, the most extraordinary sight met her eyes. The front of the tunnel and part of the surrounding hill had been completely blown away. And from the opening a great gush of water, thick and solid, was spouting out into the sea.

It had worked! Jane was so excited she found that she was jumping up and down and shouting. Then she sat and watched while the flood waters rushed from Curl Valley. Sometimes she saw tree trunks thrown out, once a farm cart, and once, for three minutes the water suddenly stopped altogether and then, with a great spurt, a whole haystack shot like a bullet out of the hole, landed, and slowly floated away.

All this was slowly beginning to turn the sea a dark brown colour, and gradually the chunks of hay and branches of trees and other pieces of flotsam and jetsam covered it like a strange fleet. But it grew too dark to see these, and then difficult to see the long, thick hosepipe of water springing out of the bottom of the hill; soon Jane was sitting growing colder and colder and now suddenly very tired, listening almost in a dream to the endless crashing and splashing of the water.

All at once, however, she heard a different roaring, and saw coming swiftly towards her along the beach a great pool of light. In a few moments she saw that it was a helicopter with powerful searchlights shining down. When it came opposite the tunnel it stopped and, hovering some fifty feet in the air, began to swing its searchlights in wide arcs along the beach and up and down the hillside. Suddenly one of these beams struck the place where Jane was sitting and at once, though both blinded and deafened, she sprang to her feet and began to shout and wave.

The helicopter saw her. Its engine noise softened and it sank swiftly to the ground. The next moment a fat, jolly-faced man came clumping up the hill. 'Well, you've caused us as much trouble as a sack full of monkeys, young lady,' he said when he'd reached her, 'you and that Mrs Deal. But I don't know but what you may have done a good job.'

He took her hand and led her to the helicopter. The next instant they were roaring up into the sky (rather like being in the kite, thought Jane). But, exciting as the journey was, she saw very little of it. She was so tired after the day's adventures that by the time they had risen up above the hills she had fallen asleep.

For three days the tunnel gushed, slowly emptying Curl Valley. People came from miles around to see the extraordinary sight and take photographs. By the end, when the water was no longer leaping out but racing like a river and gouging a deep channel in the shingle, over three thousand people had come to see it.

After three days the valley was empty enough for them to return. Mrs Deal who had been put to bed in her hotel bedroom, also said she felt strong enough to travel. And so on Wednesday morning, accompanied by the fat pilot, Jim, they all set off for Curl Castle in a Land-Rover.

It was a difficult journey. By no means all the water had left the valley and on all sides there were ponds and puddles and little rivers; often the road was completely covered. Several trees had been uprooted by the force of the in-pouring water, and from all the others hung festoons of grass and hay and other flotsam swept into their branches by the flood. (Luckily the farmers were all on holiday too, so no one had been drowned.) And everywhere there swirled a delicate, cold mist as, in the hot July sun, the valley slowly steamed itself dry.

But the Castle itself was an even wetter and sadder sight. As they swished up to it over the sodden lawn, they could see that all the windows had been broken and several small pieces of furniture had floated through them and then, as the waters fell again, had been deposited all over the flower bed. Smashed drainpipes hung loosely against the walls, with torn creepers drooping beside them.

But when they got inside they could hardly believe their eyes, so terrible was the confusion. The air was cold and dank, water dripped and oozed and trickled from everything, wending its way down stairs and walls to form pools and lakes in all the rooms and corridors; and all over the place, stacked in untidy, sodden heaps, lay the precious furniture, the bedclothes, brushes, pictures, vacuum cleaners, gumboots, suits of armour, in fact everything that had filled the Castle for hundreds of years.

When she saw it, and thought not just of the dusting, but of the mopping and mending and drying it would all mean, Mrs Deal sank onto a nearby sofa (though immediately springing up again when, like a large sponge, it sent jets of water in all directions), Mrs Deal leant weakly against a dripping wall, and began to moan. 'Oh dear, oh dear, oh dear, oh dear . . .' in a faint despairing voice. And Jane herself, though interested in the disaster, wondered what on earth they were to do.

Luckily, however, Jim at once took charge. 'First,' he said, 'we must make a list of what we'll need. Then I'll get on the blower to camp and see if the CO can send some trucks out with some of the boys. Now you cheer up, Mrs Deal,' he went on, 'you have a cup of tea and you'll soon be as right as rain.' Though it seemed a tactless comparison in the circumstances, Jane liked him for his kindness, and Mrs Deal at once brightened.

They squelched their way up to the roof and while Mrs Deal bustled about with the primus stove, Jim and Jane made a long list of what they would need: oil for the central heating, all the servants to return at once, food, mops, cloths, dusters, buckets, carpenters, window-menders, builders – the list soon covered several sheets of paper. Then after they had finished their tea, they each took some of the list and went to separate telephones to send telegrams and instructions. The great battle to restore Curl Castle had begun.

At first Jane was very busy. All her toy-cupboards had to be gone through and everything ruined by the flood thrown away. She made out a list of all the new clothes she would need. She wrote a long letter to her father and mother describing exactly what had happened, with a lot of pencil drawings showing Mrs Deal falling down the stairs under the piano, she (Jane) blowing up the tunnel, the helicopter, etc.

But after a week she suddenly realized that she hadn't anything very much more to do. The servants were too busy to talk, and had also left all their children behind with relations, so she still had no one to play with; the builders and decorators and insurance men were interesting to watch for a while, but only for a while; and Mrs Deal had started, once the first rooms were dry, on a frenzy of dusting so violent that it was dangerous to approach her. Jane decided that the time had come to pay another visit to the Book and this, on the Wednesday after they had returned, and after a large and delicious lunch, she accordingly did.

THE journey to the old library took very much longer than it had the first time. The vacuum cleaners were all at the menders, and even if they hadn't been, all the carpets had been taken up and hung out to dry. It was a gloomy walk after she left the workmen, the only sound her footsteps echoing on the damp floorboards and from the ruined, dripping rooms.

After an hour she reached the familiar, brass-knobbed door. Once again it swung easily open, once more she found herself on the dark twisting staircase. A few moments later she was standing in the library again.

At first she thought it was all the same. But in fact,

she soon noticed that two rather strange things had happened. The first was that the steps, which she was quite sure she had left under the hole after her return from the Tunnellers, had been moved back into the middle of the library.

However, the possibilities of ghosts – or worse – which this at once suggested were so worrying, that Jane quickly turned instead to the Book. And here she got another surprise. Because instead of the square in the town, where an old man was about to be executed, which she was almost sure had been the first picture last time, she now found a very detailed drawing of some mermaids swimming about on the edge of a waterfall. Nor, as she turned the pages, could she find any trace of the picture of Kronin, though once a glimpse of some high mountains reminded her of the Tunneller's country.

She looked at several pictures – one of spiders, one of some large bats flying across a lake, and one of what looked like a giant's grocer shop – but none of them looked quite safe. Then all at once she came on one which seemed to consist entirely of flowers. They were so bright and cheerful, so soft looking, that she felt nothing could possibly go wrong in a land which had such lovely things in it.

Rather nervously Jane crawled out and sat beside a large poppy. Then she took the piece of carefully folded paper out of the pocket of her jeans, and said very quickly:

'Shut eyes, do not look,
Close your pages on me Book.'

At once the thick paper began to turn into that cotton

wool which Jane remembered before. The picture faded and became milky, and her legs began slowly to sink. She held her breath and shut her eyes, and once again, had there been anyone else in the library, they would have been surprised to see the giant cover of the Book rise up and close swiftly down, driving the little girl like a nail into the page.

Jane found that she was sitting on a small bank covered in big bright flowers. Beside her grew the poppy, quite as large, if not larger than it had seemed a moment before. When Jane stood up it was level with her chest, and each red, tissue-papery petal was the size of her hand.

The bank was at the edge of a wide, moss-covered track twisting through a forest of enormous trees. From many of the higher branches long creepers dangled to the ground and everywhere, on the creepers, the large green leaves, swooping among the giant flowers, millions of gaily coloured birds chirruped and called, filling the air with their song. There were also other noises coming from the forest which she thought might be monkeys. 'Perhaps,' thought Jane, as she set off down the track, 'I'm in the jungles of Africa or South America.'

Certainly it was warm enough. A faint mist rose from the soft damp moss and Jane soon rolled up the sleeves of her shirt. Though the track was very flat and smooth (she thought it odd there were no stones) she had to clamber over lots of branches. After an hour of walking in the hot sun, she decided to rest. She had hardly sat down on a fallen tree when she began to have the curious feeling she was being watched. She looked about her, but could see nothing but the birds who twittered everywhere. And then, just at her feet, she heard a gentle click – click – click – click, like a tiny pair of knitting needles.

She found that one of the smallest birds she had ever seen was perched beside her, staring at her with bright, black eyes. It was the size of a small bumble bee, with shiny blue wings and a pointed beak like a pin. It was so light that it hardly bent the stem of grass on which it swayed. And it seemed completely unafraid of Jane, because when she slowly stretched out her hand it hopped easily on to her little finger and perched there as she lifted it to her face.

'Hullo,' said Jane.

Click – click went the bird.

'I suppose you *are* a bird,' said Jane, and then because she had been feeling rather lonely and wanted to go on talking, she went on, 'Do you know where I could get a drink? I feel so hot and thirsty.' At once the bird, or bumble bird, rose swiftly into the air and poised hovering in front of her face. Then it darted off again and all the time made such a clicking with its pointed, pin-like beak, that she soon realized it wished her to follow. She, therefore, set off after it down the track.

They had not gone far when the bumble bird turned up a little path to the left and, after following this for a while, they came to a little glade. It was filled with tall white lilies, whose large waxy flowers pointed upwards like wine glasses. The bumble bird balanced on the nearest of these and when Jane came up, she saw that the flower, indeed all the lilies, were filled with a pale liquid the colour of weak tea. The bumble bird now made dipping movements and clicked rapidly at her.

'All right,' said Jane. And bending forward she tipped the flower into her mouth.

It was delicious. Jane was reminded of a very fresh melon, only sparkling and not too sweet. She drank six flower cups and was just about to drink the seventh (out of greed, not thirst) when suddenly she began to feel very drowsy. She gave a great yawn and turning to the bumble bird she said 'Aaaaaaah – dear bumble bird, I think ... must just ... goodnight,' and lying comfortably back into the moss, shut her eyes, and in a moment was fast asleep.

The bumble bird flew down close to her face, hovered there for a few seconds, then shot into the air and flew at great speed into the trees.

Jane was woken some hours later by a delicate pecking on the nose. It was the bumble bird again. But when she had rubbed her eyes and sat up, she saw that standing watching her was a boy of about her own age, leaning calmly against a tree. When he saw that she was awake, he smiled at her and said, 'Did you have a good dreamless sleep?'

'Very good, thank you,' said Jane, 'but I think I was put to sleep by these flowers. What are they?'

'Surely you've seen Deluna before,' said the boy, 'we take them every night to stop dreams. What do you take?'

'When I can't sleep my mother gives me an aspirin,' said Jane, 'if I still can't sleep they give me two aspirins. Ten aspirins,' she added, 'is a fatal dose.'

'Ah well, I expect in different parts they have different names,' said the boy, 'but you don't know my name. I'm called Tamil and I live half an hour away in Fluffball.'

'My name is Jane,' said Jane, 'and I live in Curl Castle.'

'Curl Castle?' said Tamil, 'I don't think I've ever heard of that village. But of course the jungle is very large. You must have travelled a long way. Why not come and spend the night in our house. Where are you going?'

'Deal Village,' said Jane, 'miles away. You won't have heard of it.'

'Miles?' said Tamil, 'surely you mean hours?'

'Oh, not hours,' said Jane quickly, 'weeks away, months, years I think. Yes, at least eight years away.'

'Goodness,' said Tamil, looking at her with admiration, 'eight years away. They never told me the jungle was that big. You must talk to the Aged. He will be very interested.' Jane felt that the conversation was getting out of control, so she said, 'Let's go to your house now. I'm beginning to feel rather hungry.'

As they walked, she was able to look at him more closely without appearing to stare. He had a kind, rather thin face, with fair hair and black eyes. His skin was a deep brown from the sun and he was quite naked except for a strip of light green cotton tied round his waist.

It was plain that Tamil was also thinking about her, because all at once he said, 'Curl Castle and Deal Village. Do tell me why you are going such a very long way.'

For a moment Jane didn't answer. As with the Tunneller Kronin, she felt rather nervous of explaining exactly how she had arrived. At the same time what she had said seemed likely to lead to more and more embarrassing questions. She particularly didn't want to meet the Aged, who sounded like a very grown up grown-up. Also, like Kronin, Tamil seemed gentle and kind. So she stopped and said 'Look, I'm afraid I didn't exactly tell the exact truth about Curl Castle and Deal Village.'

'Oh?' said Tamil, 'why not?'

'Well, the thing is,' began Jane. And then, as quickly as she could, she told him everything that had happened.

When she had finished, Tamil looked at the ground and said slowly, 'I see. Now I understand. I think I won't tell my mother and father, not of course that they'd mind. I'll just say you're a traveller.'

'How do you mean "You understand"?' said Jane, 'am I odd or something? What do you understand?' As with Kronin, she had the impression that her arrival through the Book meant something to him which he didn't want to tell her.

'Oh, not odd,' said Tamil, laughing. 'You're very lucky, really. But I don't really know very much about it. In any case you'll find out sometime and it's certainly nothing to worry about.'

And with that Jane had to be content, because Tamil went on to say that it was getting late. As they walked, he told Jane about his country. It was called Tree Land, but was in fact not really 'land' at all. Tamil explained that the trees they saw around them were thousands of years old, but most of what they saw were only the tops of those trees. What had happened was that the trees grew so close together that when branches fell they got caught and entangled with other branches before they reached the ground, these in turn caught other branches and soon a sort of floor had been formed many feet above the ground. Seeds had landed in crevices of this floor, had grown into flowers, then died, to rot down gradually into earth. More seeds had fallen, more branches, and over hundreds of years the floor had grown many feet thick, able to support whole trees on its own, and these too had fallen, rotted down and made the floor even thicker and stronger. Then sometime long before anyone remembered, Tamil's ancestors had climbed up the giant trees from the jungle below and had found this sunny land, full of richly growing flowers and no enemies, and had lived there ever since.

'Do you mean that we are really walking on a sort of platform?' said Jane in amazement, looking down at the solid-looking earth and moss of the track at her feet, 'you mean that somewhere underneath is a gap and then below that the real earth? But we might fall through.'

'Oh we'd never fall through,' said Tamil, 'it's far too thick for that. The Aged says it is fifty feet thick even at the thinnest part, and it is all bound together by roots and huge old tree trunks.'

'But what happens down at the bottom, where the trees grow from? Who lives there?' asked Jane.

'Nobody knows,' said Tamil. 'To tell you the truth I wouldn't ask anyone if I were you. We aren't really meant to talk about it. If you do ask people they look very frightened and quickly change the subject. I'm about the only person in our village who isn't frightened – well, me and my friend Mayna. One day when we are bigger we are going to climb down one of the holes and explore. But it's very dangerous. There have been men who have explored but none have ever come back. The name of down there is the Land of Dreams.'

While they had been talking the track had gradually been widening, and now it opened into a large clearing. All round the edges were about thirty little houses made from large leaves plaited together. In the middle was a much larger house, standing on stilts and made out of tree trunks. 'That's where the Aged lives,' said Tamil.

The village was a peaceful and happy sight in the evening sun. In front of each little house sat women sewing and talking, and everywhere little brown children were playing and laughing.

'First you should pay your respects to the Aged,' said Tamil.

'Oh dear, must I?' said Jane. 'I feel so shy.'

'Well, not tonight then. But before you go. It's our custom. Now, come with me and meet my family.'

First Jane was introduced to Tamil's mother, a smiling woman with her fair hair tied in a bun and a rather large nose. Then she met his five little sisters. His mother gave her a bowl of grey, porridge-like stuff, with some syrup and pieces of very good fresh bread and jam.

After this, though she longed to go on asking Tamil questions about Tree Land and the land of Dreams, he said she should go to bed.

'We get up with the sun here,' he said, 'and go to bed with it as well. So you see it is already late.' Then he showed Jane where she was to sleep, which was in a large wickerwork hammock swinging from the ceiling in a tiny room off the main one. She said goodnight and had just settled herself in it with a blanket over her, when a shape blocked out the dim light from the door.

It was Tamil's mother. 'I've brought you some Deluna,' she said, 'in case you dream. Tamil said you wouldn't need it, but there's no need to waste your own remedies while staying with us. Come drink it up and you'll have a lovely, dreamless night.'

Jane thought it would be rude to refuse, so she thanked Tamil's mother and once again tasted the sweet, pale liquid she had drunk from the lilies. A few minutes later she slipped into a deep and, as it turned out, completely dreamless sleep.

The next morning, as they wandered among the paths and long, narrow fields which surrounded the village, Tamil answered Jane's many questions about Tree Land.

'I don't see any rivers,' said Jane, 'or fountains or ponds. How do you get water?'

'Look,' said Tamil. He ran a few steps down the path they were following to one of the many banks of dark green moss which were at its edge. Stuffing his hands into it he pulled off a large chunk and then squeezed it. At once water poured onto the path. 'That's one way,' he said, 'the other is the water plants, which are like the Deluna lilies only bigger and filled with water.'

Although Tamil told her a great deal about Tree Land – about its peaceful peoples, it's animals, the great rains which sometimes swept it – there was one thing he did not speak of, and after a while Jane decided she must ask about it.

'If it worries you, Tamil,' she said, 'of course, I'll quite understand. But I would like to know a little more about the Land of Dreams.'

For a moment she thought she saw a shadow of nervousness cross his face, but he answered quickly enough. 'Well, the thing is I don't really know any more than I've told you. This other land may not exist – it's only a sort of legend really – a story. But it's true that explorers have gone to find it and have never returned. It's true, we're not allowed to talk about it. And it's true that in secret parts of the forest there are deep holes which lead no one knows where. If you like, I could show you one after lunch.'

'Oh please do,' said Jane, 'yes, in fact I'm getting quite hungry now.'

Lunch, consisting of hot, sweet black porridge and some sugared violet petals, was soon over. Tamil told his mother that he was going to take Jane for a walk in the jungle and, after collecting his friend Mayna, they set off.

Mayna was shorter and fatter than Tamil, with a happy smiling face, and as they walked he skipped ahead and came running back, laughing and making jokes. But as they plunged deeper and deeper into the jungle, and as the paths grew narrower, the light dimmer, even he became quiet. Soon all three were struggling in silence through thick undergrowth.

They had pushed on in this way for about half an hour when Tamil suddenly stopped and whispered, 'Listen.'

Jane could at first hear nothing, but then very faintly came the sound of running, or really dripping, water.

'We're nearly there,' whispered Tamil.

A few more clambering steps, and then the bushes suddenly stopped and they were looking down into a small hollow. There was not much light, but in the middle of the hollow, Jane could see the blackness of a deep hole. From out of this hole rose the trunk of a huge tree, and from its depths came the sound of trickling water they had heard a moment before.

'There you are,' whispered Tamil, 'that's it.'

'Have you ever tried to get down it,' said Jane, 'I mean even a little way?'

'No, no,' said Tamil, 'it's far too dangerous. We've only been here twice before.' Looking at them clinging to the bushes at the edge, staring down with wide eyes, Jane suddenly realized that both the boys were very frightened.

'But it looks easy,' she said, 'look, you can see that the branches of that tree going down in the middle could easily be climbed.'

'No, no,' said Tamil nervously, 'far too dangerous. Look, do you see that steam coming from the hole,' and as he mentioned it Jane could see that there were faint wisps of steam rising sluggishly in the dim light, 'it must be very hot down there. You'd probably be boiled alive.'

'Or eaten by huge ants,' said Mayna, 'or squashed by worms. Look, we'd better get back. It's already late.'

And then Jane made up her mind. 'Listen, Tamil,' she said, 'I'm going to explore that hole. I can quite easily get to the edge by those roots and things and then jump across to the tree. You know it's all right for me. If there is any danger I can just say the magic words and return home. If there is no danger then I can really find out what happens down there.'

'No you can't, you mustn't,' said Tamil.

'Now don't worry,' said Jane, forbidding though the hole looked. If I don't come back in ten minutes go and explain to your mother that I decided to go on with my journey.' And before the boys could stop her, she had leapt lightly down, stepped from branch and root to the edge of the hole and then jumped easily onto one of the branches growing out of the trunk of the tree. 'Goodbye Tamil, goodbye Mayna,' she called, 'see you soon.' And before the nervousness she already felt could get too strong she at once began to climb down into the dark, earth-smelling hole. As she disappeared, she heard faintly from above her, 'Goodbye Jane. Be careful. Goodbye.'

At first Jane found it quite easy to climb down the tree. There were a great many branches and footholds which, although it soon became completely dark, she easily found by feeling; and for some reason the earth through which the tree rose never came very close to the trunk. The air was warm and damp and the earth smelt rich and rotten like a forest floor in summer time. 'It must smell like this to worms and moles,' she thought.

But as she climbed deeper the trickling water began to pour onto her in little rivulets. Soon she was soaked to the skin. The earth pressed closer and closer and she had to push her way down through dead branches and matted, sweet-smelling leaves. Several times she became completely stuck and only the most violent kicking and jumping enabled her to get any further.

It was when she became finally stuck, that Jane realized how unlikely Tamil's story was. Another world *underneath* Tree Land indeed! All she had done was to burrow deep into the ground in this boggy hole and now would either have to remain there till she drowned or suffocated, or say the rhyme and return to Curl Castle. Furiously she gave a kick at the criss-crossed branches and earth around her feet.

To her horror, with a sudden cracking and rush, they disappeared. One moment they were there, the next Jane felt the ground fall beneath her. Wildly she grabbed at the tree, for a moment held to a slender, slippery branch, then as it snapped felt herself falling into deep, dark, space – falling . . . falling . . . falling . . .

JANE dropped like a stone for about five seconds; then to her surprise she found that she was falling more and more slowly. The air around her was becoming thicker and thicker until very soon it supported her as though she floated in an invisible sea.

Jane also realized that she was moving. The air nudged and buffeted at her back, and once her hand touched a slimy tree trunk sliding past. The current gradually grew stronger and before long she was being carried through the darkness quite fast, the air swirling between her legs and turning her slowly over and over like a leaf in the wind.

Although it was not unpleasant, Jane was relieved

when she saw it growing lighter ahead. Soon tall tree trunks began to appear on either side, looming out of the fog which was blowing Jane between them. It became lighter every moment; now Jane could see the ground below, now see she was floating down towards it. The fog became a mist, the mist melted away, and suddenly, light as thistledown, she landed on her feet again. Looking back she could see only a deepening fog, with the trees rising straight up until they disappeared into the darkness; but ahead, she saw the edge of the jungle, with sunlight shining through the trees and beyond, the green of meadows. Fifty steps, a small ditch to be jumped, and she was out in the sun, suddenly surprised at the noise of birds.

After a pause to wipe off the mud which still clung to her sandals from forcing her way through the floor of Tree Land, and to wring as much water from her clothes as she could, Jane hurried off towards a distant hill.

The countryside was surprisingly English, with little fields and hedges not unlike those round Curl Castle. After half an hour, Jane turned to look back at the jungle. The trees rose, straight and branchless, so high into the sky that she had to tilt her head back to look towards their tops. But these, and therefore the second level which was Tree Land, were hidden far above the clouds.

She was now beginning to feel extremely hungry. She had just reached an oak tree growing in the middle of the fourth field she had crossed. It was surrounded by little oak apples and Jane suddenly murmured to herself, 'I wonder if I could eat oak apples.'

'Of course you could,' said a voice behind her, 'if that's why you are here.'

Very surprised, Jane looked up. Sitting on one of the branches was a short, but extremely fat little man wearing a bowler hat. Next to him sat an equally fat little woman in a large, old-fashioned, orange bathing dress. The man was in pyjamas and dressing-gown. As Jane continued to stare at them, the woman said, 'Introduce me to the young lady, Mr Henry.'

'Of course, dear,' said Mr Henry, 'how remiss. I would like you to meet Mrs Forth, my wife. My dear I would like to introduce you to Miss . . . Miss . . . Miss . . .?' He inclined his round fat head politely towards her and lifted his bowler hat.

But Jane's manners had completely disappeared with amazement. 'How ever did you get up there?' she said.

'Ah, you think we are too fat?' said Mr Henry quickly, 'granted, granted. We are fat, very fat, but we're also incredibly light. Observe.' And pushing himself off the branch, Mr Henry rose lightly into the air and then very slowly floated down until he came to rest beside Jane, where he continued to bob up and down like a balloon in a hot drawing-room. Looking up he called to his wife. 'Show her, my dear.'

At once a silly but pleased expression spread over Mrs Forth's round face. She too propelled herself into the air, but on her way down, merely by raising one plump, pink leg, she turned a complete somersault.

'How extraordinary,' said Jane.

'Hardly extraordinary,' said Mr Henry, 'this is what we want. This way we combine the cosiness, the jollyness, the warmth and lovely, rubbery softness of being fat without any of the disadvantages. We never get breathless, my wife's feet never ache, furniture never breaks and we eat and eat and eat. All because we are so delightfully light. How much do you think I weigh?'

Jane looked at him. A ton? To be polite she said, 'Fifteen stone.'

'I weigh two ounces,' said Mr Henry grandly; 'we both weigh two ounces. Now hold out both your hands.' Then Mr Henry turned to his wife, 'Come my dear, let us show this nice young lady some more of our little games.' And with a 'hurr-up' they both leapt daintily into the air and came lightly down on Jane's out-stretched palms. Neither of them seemed heavier than a hard-boiled egg. With a gentle movement, Jane threw them both up into the air, and when they had once more bobbed to rest beside her, said 'But how do you do it? Does everyone round here do it?'

'Only if they really want to,' said Mr Henry, 'why we met a man the other night, well how can I describe him? He was as thin as a bootlace. Now, he wanted to be heavy. Every step he took he sank up to his thighs; we saw him break a large rock into fragments just by sitting on it. Now, you want something to eat. Why not try the oak apples or a branch? What would you like them to taste of?'

'Fish fingers,' said Jane.

'Well, try one,' said Mr Henry.

But before Jane could bend to pick one up, there came a faint cry of 'Mr Henry' from some way off.

While they had been talking, a faint breeze had sprung up and this had carried Mrs Forth a considerable distance out into the field and was rapidly carrying her farther.

'Mr Henry,' she called, 'we shall be late for breakfast.'

Mr Henry, who had only kept his position by holding fast to one of the branches of the oak, from which he now waved like a large flag, turned his head and cried 'Coming, my love.' And then said hurriedly to Jane, 'She's quite right. If you're late for breakfast you never catch up. Well goodbye, Miss . . . Miss . . .?'

'Jane,' said Jane, not bothering about Lady.

'Goodbye, Miss Jane.'

'Goodbye,' called Jane, as, releasing his hold, Mr Henry was swept away, his dressing gown billowing around him. She watched him join his wife and then saw them hand in hand begin a series of huge, slow leaps, the last of which must have taken them up into some stronger currents of wind, because they were almost immediately blown out of sight.

Although it seemed odd that they should worry about being late for breakfast in the late afternoon, unless of course they had a long way to travel, Jane now felt too hungry to worry about Mr Henry and Mrs Forth. Instead she picked up one of the dead branches lying at the foot of the oak tree and took a dainty nibble from one end.

It did not surprise her to find that it tasted exactly like one of Mrs Deal's best fish fingers, only cold. '*Hot* please,' thought Jane; and at once had to drop the branch as it began to sizzle in her fingers. She soon found that by concentrating she could make anything taste of anything. Grass of chicken, bark of chocolate, earth, poured from her cupped hands, became milk as it entered her mouth. After a large and varied meal of chicken, chocolate, ham, cheese fingers, fish fingers, summer pudding, milk, bitter lemon, sherbet, roast mutton and chewing gum, Jane set off again in the direction of the hill.

The field was surrounded by a high hedge full of gaps. On the other side of it was a grassy path which, though it twisted and turned seemed to lead more or less towards the hill. Jane decided to follow it.

After an hour's hard walking, the path grew wider and wider, the hedges lower, and before long both disappeared and Jane found she was standing at the top of a shallow valley, looking across to the little hill. It was becoming dark and a cold breeze had blown up from the valley which, in the gloom of the evening and with its scattered rocks, looked most uninviting. Nor was there yet any sign of a village or indeed of any human beings at all; in fact the countryside was growing visibly more wild and frightening. However, having decided to reach the top of the hill, Jane could think of nothing better to do. It was still true that if there *were* any villages then she would most easily see them from there.

Accordingly she set off, jumping over the stones and little rocks and walking round the larger ones, until all at once she thought she heard voices. She stopped and listened. They had come from the left, but had been very faint.

'Hullooooo,' shouted Jane, 'is there anybody there?' No one answered.

'I'm *sure* I heard voices,' thought Jane, and climbing

onto a nearby boulder she was about to shout again into the gloomy valley when she saw a slowly moving figure coming towards her.

It was a little girl of about her own age. As she walked she looked at the ground and put one foot carefully in front of the other in the way Jane herself often did when she was pretending to walk on a tightrope.

'Hullo,' Jane called excitedly.

The little girl looked up, waved, and then looked down again. As she came nearer, Jane was interested to see that she was wearing the same jeans as she was. Also she had the same short hair, which now hung over her face as she walked on her tightrope. Not until she was quite close, and Jane had again said 'hullo,' did she look up. And then Jane saw the most remarkable sight. She found that she was looking at herself.

The little girl was not just rather like her, or reminded her of her, or could have been her sister – she was *exactly* like her. She had the same nose, the same eyes and mouth and teeth; she had a mole where Jane had a mole and a tiny mark on her throat where Jane had a mark. She *was* Jane.

Jane stared at her, and she looked back at Jane, though without nearly as much interest. She had one eye with a speck in it like Jane did, and her parting was on the left.

'Who are you?' said Jane at last.

'Jane Charrington,' said the little girl.

'But you *can't* be,' said Jane, 'I'm Jane Charrington. At least, you may be as well. It must be a coincidence. But we look exactly alike.'

'How do you do,' said the other Jane, smiling kindly.

Jane took her hand and shook it. It fitted exactly, and they gave, she noticed, exactly the same number of shakes.

'I know,' said Jane, 'you're my identical twin. Are you an orphan? Have you never seen our mother?'

'I've never seen my mother,' said the other Jane.

'But you *must*,' said Jane, 'how did you get here? I never knew I had a sister. You must have been stolen away from hospital and Mummy doesn't even know about you.'

'Well, I don't know about that,' said the other Jane, 'after all, there are quite a lot of us.' And now Jane saw that they were being joined by other figures emerging from behind the rocks and arriving, in fact, from all directions. And all of them were wearing jeans and shirts, all of them had short brown hair and brown eyes and moles and marks on their throat. All of them were Janes.

'This is Jane Charrington,' said the first Jane as they came up, and each one said, 'How do you do? I'm Jane Charrington.' And for a while the air was full of Jane Charrington, Jane Charrington, how do you do, I'm Jane Charrington, Charrington, Charrington, Charrington.'

'But you *can't* be,' shouted Jane tearfully, 'we can't be. We can't all be the same person.' Suddenly she began to feel very frightened and strange. She wanted to cry, and then run to Mrs Deal or her mother.

'Do you know Mrs Deal?' she said, 'do you know Curl Castle?'

'Well, *she* knows Mrs Deal,' said one of the Janes pointing to another Jane, 'but of course I'm very good at English.'

'So am I,' said Jane; 'yes, that's true.'

'But I'm very bad at maths,' said yet another Jane.

'So am I,' said Jane.

'I like fish fingers,' 'I tell myself stories in bed,' 'I can swim,' 'I want to go to school.' All the Janes were speaking at once (and there now seemed to be about three hundred of them), and the noise grew so loud that Jane, the real Jane, suddenly felt she would go mad if they didn't stop.

'IT'S ALL TRUE,' she shouted, 'I'M LIKE THAT TOO.'

At once there was complete silence. Jane had a strong feeling that no one liked her. At last the first Jane said quietly 'You can't be. No one is *all* the Jane Charringtons. I *only* walk on a tightrope and Jane over there is the *only* Jane who tells herself stories.'

'And I'm *only* bad at maths,' said another Jane.

'And I wouldn't *dream* of pretending I knew what Jane meant when she said Curl Castle,' said another, 'I only talk about Mrs Deal and her dusting.'

And suddenly, in the middle of a muttering chorus of 'I *only* . . . I wouldn't . . . I'm the Jane who . . .' one of the Janes pushed through and gave her a violent push on the place where she had once broken her arm.

'Ow,' cried Jane, jumping back, 'that's my sore place. That's where I broke my arm.'

At once the Jane who had pinched her shouted, 'SHE'S SAYING SHE HAD *MY* BROKEN ARM. SHE'S PRETENDING SHE'S *ALL* THE JANES. WE MUST KILL HER.'

'I'm not, I'm not,' cried Jane, 'I'm Jane Charrington of Curl Castle. I'm *not* pretending.'

But the crowd of Janes just seemed to become angrier. They began to mutter louder and louder, to crowd closer and hold out their hands, their little hands so exactly like hers; and all at once Jane found that she had turned round and was running as fast as she could away from them towards the hill.

It was now much darker. The rocks appeared suddenly out of the shadows and had to be jumped or dodged. But though Jane could hear all the other Janes running along behind, she realized that probably only one of them would be able to run as fast as her. And in fact, when she looked hurriedly back, she saw that none of them were yet gaining.

But although they could not run any faster, they certainly knew the way better. Three, four, five times she tripped and each time they drew closer. Suddenly, quite close, she saw a Jane rushing towards her from the left, and when she swerved to the right, another Jane appeared yelling and waving a stone which she at once threw at Jane with all her might.

Jane tripped again, and then again. Loud cries of triumph came from all sides. She scrambled up and ran panting on, but now she heard the sound of feet close behind and stones began to whizz past as the awful pack of little girls threw and shouted and threw again.

Just as she was about to give up in despair, Jane saw in front of her a flight of stairs. They rose straight out of the ground, and without thinking she rushed up them.

Twenty stairs. But as she reached the top, another twenty appeared before her. And as she ran up them, another twenty. From the ground, as she climbed, there came a great roar of rage.

Looking back, Jane saw that, as fast as she climbed, the stairs disappeared behind her. Now, gathered in the last evening light, a vast circle of little girls looked up to where she stood on the staircase in the air above them. They were jumping and shouting and, suddenly feeling that they were not, in fact, really like her at all, Jane called down, 'Shut up. You are all just dreams. I am the real Jane Charrington. Not you.' Then, ignoring the yells and shouts, she began to climb the staircase as it appeared before her, turning back every now and again to make sure it was disappearing behind, and had not suddenly shot down to earth to allow her terrible pursuers to start their chase again.

Jane climbed as fast as she could because she hoped that the stairs would soon reach somewhere. But the higher she climbed, the emptier seemed the evening sky, and the dizzier she grew. The valley was just a vague dot in the gloom and soon it had disappeared altogether. Then all at once Jane stumbled and had she not seized the stairs would have fallen to a hideous death on the rocks below. Luckily just after this the stairs became a moving staircase and she was able to sit down and let herself be carried swiftly higher.

As she rose, it grew much lighter because the sun had still not set at that enormous height, and in its light Jane saw that at last the stairs seemed to have some object in their climb. They were approaching a vast cloud, miles long, which hovered pinkly above them. They drew rapidly closer. Soon they had plunged into its thick, damp folds. But still the stairs went on; indeed they seemed to move even faster and for so long that Jane became quite wet and expected any second to pop out of the top of the cloud.

At last they stopped. At the same time, the cloud became a little thinner and Jane saw that she had arrived at the walls of some large though, because of the cloud, dim building. Its walls were made of steel and were entirely smooth except for a small door against which the top of the stairs now rested. As she walked towards this, it slid silently open and Jane quickly stepped through. The door at once shut itself behind her.

She was in a short, brightly lit tunnel, with curved steel walls which reflected her in the oddest shapes, like looking into a spoon. Jane followed this to its end and there, where it divided, found a notice saying 'Visitors This Way'. Several times the tunnel divided and each time there was a similar notice, until eventually she came to another sliding door saying 'Visitors' Lift'. The door, as she had expected, opened as she came to it and shut behind her.

The lift was very small, with a small red stool in its corner. One wall was covered with 994 buttons – each numbered – and the 995th button had an arrow pointing at it saying 'Visitors' Button'.

She pressed it and immediately the lift shot upwards with a purring sound. Each time they passed a floor there was a little ping. In four minutes, nineteen seconds the lift stopped at the 995th floor and Jane stepped out into a large, round room.

Opposite her, in a curved steel chair, was a tall, elderly man with thick grey hair, bright brown eyes and very fuzzy eyebrows. He was wearing a white silk dressing-gown and purple pyjamas.

'Welcome, my dear,' he said in a deep, kindly voice. 'You must be tired and hungry. Come and sit down.' He led her over to a smaller steel chair opposite his own, and went on, 'Now before I satisfy your curiosity, I shall order some food. What would you like to eat?'

Jane found that she was not in the least shy of the kind man. After thinking a moment, she said 'Could I have some fried eggs, fried bread and bacon and a glass of Lucozade, please.'

The man pressed a button on his chair and speaking into mid-air, repeated her order. 'Won't be long,' he said, smiling at her.

The round room had no windows and only one door. There was a thick, woolly rug on the floor. In front of the man a large desk stuck out of the wall, and this was covered with buttons, dials, telephones, switches, levers, and, in the middle, a round television screen. After looking carefully at everything, Jane said 'Perhaps if it's not rude to ask, you could begin to satisfy my curiosity *before* my supper arrives.' But as she spoke there came a soft ping and a little table rose up in front of her laden with food.

'Of course,' said the man, 'now you have a good meal and I'll explain while you eat.'

'You have come,' he began, 'to what you would call the capital of the Land of Dreams.

'Here we make dreams and send them out to everyone who sleeps. When you've finished eating I'll take you round and show you how it works. I am the Dream Master. Once, when dreams were made by hand, I was very busy, solving problems, inventing dreams for prophets, priests and so on, but now that everything is done by electric brains and computers, I don't really have quite enough to do.'

'I see,' said Jane, who didn't exactly see. 'Do you mean that everyone in the world who dreams, has their dream made here?'

'Everyone,' said the Dream Master, 'we are a very large organization.'

'And those people I saw on my way here,' said Jane, 'were they people dreaming, or am I really asleep and is all this my dream?'

'Oh, you're awake all right,' said the Dream Master, 'the people you saw were dreaming. As I remember you passed through part of the Hopeful Country, where people dream of what they hope will happen. Except when you went into a Nightmare Valley and had a small nightmare.'

'But where *are* we?' said Jane, who was becoming more and more puzzled. 'Do people who fall asleep come a long way and have their dreams here? If so, what happens to their bodies?'

'It's difficult to explain,' said the Dream Master, 'in fact I wouldn't worry about it. You see the Land of Dreams or Dream Land, is everywhere, but people can only see it and enter it when asleep. To find it when awake, as you have done, is much more complicated and very rarely happens. Now look,' the Dream Master pressed a switch on the desk and at once the steel wall of the room grew paler and paler until it had become like glass.

Jane, who had finished her supper, stood and looked. They were at the top of a very tall tower. Below them, sticking out from its bottom like the spokes of an enor-

mous wheel, nine long steel buildings stretched into the
distance. The cloud through which Jane had arrived was
all around the Dream capital, but seemed to be kept
back as though by an invisible wall.

'Each of those buildings is thirty miles long,' said the
Dream Master pointing down, 'each one makes and
sends out a certain sort of dream. That one, for instance,
is the Dream-of-the-Future factory, that one Night-
mares, that one Dreams of Food and Love. Often, of
course, people's dreams are very mixed. Then each factory sends part of the dream to this tower and it is made
up and sent from here.'

Jane looked down at the strange scene. She didn't
really understand it at all, but she had noticed that ever
since she had arrived in Dream Land nothing had surprised her in the least. Mr and Mrs Forth, even the
appearance of all the other Janes had seemed quite
normal. And so, although what the Dream Master was
saying was most mysterious, she found that she was
quite ready to believe it without understanding it. However, because it always seemed rude to say nothing when
people explained things, she tried to think of an intelli-
gent question.

'What happens if two people dream the same dream?'
she asked.

'Exactly the same dream is very rare,' said the Dream
Master, 'though it sometimes happens to twins, and
people very much in love. As a matter of fact I believe
you met two people on your way here who both have the
same dream every night. Now I'll show you round.'

They walked together over to the lift and soon found
themselves walking down a long steel corridor. It was

rather like a hospital, with shut doors on either side, each with a green light above it. From time to time men in white dressing-gowns and green pyjamas came out of the doors carrying notebooks or armfuls of steel tins. When they saw the Dream Master they bowed low and waited till he and Jane had passed.

'The steel tins you see those men carrying hold dreams which have been dreamed and are going to be put into storage. We keep all dreams, of course, for ever.'

'Could you show me some of my old dreams?' asked Jane.

'Easily,' said the Dream Master, 'though you'll find your own old dreams don't often interest you any more. But it's rather fun looking at really old dreams. Some of the Biblical ones are tremendous. I watched Potipher and Joseph again only the other day. And of course Jacob dreamt a great deal. I'll show you some.'

He did. He showed her lots of dreams all over the world (except those of people she knew, which wasn't allowed). He showed her how dreams were made and let her make some. He showed her the old equipment – coloured powder, spinning dream wheels, crystal globes – which had been used before the electric brains, lasers and other modern machinery had been put into the Dream capital. But at last he said that he had work to do and that they must return to the tower.

When they were once more sitting opposite each other in the round room, there was a short silence. Then slowly he leant forward and took both her hands in his. She saw that his kind brown eyes were very serious and that he had bent his thick eyebrows into a grave frown.

'Before you go, my child,' he said, 'I shall give you some words of warning and advice. You must listen very carefully.

'Visitors to Dream Land are very rare. Though many people have dreams, very few people have the vision to dream and stay awake. You are one of them. The last visitor we had of your age was a little girl nearly two hundred years ago. She . . . but no, I won't tell you what happened to her. I think you may one day find out.

'But, and this is the point, if you are to return to your home you must never, never while you are here, fall asleep. Not for an instant, not for a single second, however tired you are, however clever the temptations. You must not doze or even nod your head. If you do, you will be lost.

'But cheer up,' went on the Dream Master, smiling. Jane, who had certainly been rather frightened and had suddenly begun to wish she had never left Curl Castle or Mrs Deal and never opened the Book, poor Jane tried to smile back. 'I'm sure you'll be all right,' said the Dream Master, 'you are a brave girl and as long as you keep your head there's no need to worry. Good luck. And now I'm afraid you must be on your way.'

'Which way?' said Jane, looking nervously round the steel room.

'Well, I suppose I am the easiest way of all,' said the Dream Master. He walked over to the wall and leant against it.

'Goodbye,' he said.

'Goodbye,' said Jane, and then, as she watched, she saw that the Dream Master was slowly changing. Gradually a space appeared in his middle. This grew and grew and at the same time his arms and the edges of his body began to form themselves into the rocky outline of a cavern door.

As she hesitated the rocky door, or gap, suddenly spoke in the Dream Master's voice, 'Don't be afraid,' it or he boomed, 'step through me. Good luck.'

Without giving herself time to be afraid, Jane took a last look round, then stepped through and began to feel her way forward.

THE Dream-Master-door led, by way of a short passage, to another even smaller opening. As Jane groped towards it, she heard growing ever louder the sound of wind and distant thunder. A few moments later she had stepped through, and at once was almost blown flat by a great gust of cold wind.

She was standing on a stony path which, in the frequent flashes of lightning, she could see twisted away down the side of a high mountain. All round her a terrible storm was raging. Swollen black clouds sped before the continual gusts of wind, thunder rumbled and echoed and, most exciting of all, each time the lightning flicked and zipped across the sky, Jane saw quite clearly a whole wild country, with ravines and mountains and waterfalls stretched below her, and steep, craggy peaks rising above her. But when, during an especially bright flash, she turned to see the tunnel from which she had just stepped, she could see nothing. In its place was just a gulf, where the mountainside plunged into blackness.

Jane was by now quite cold and was about to hurry off down the mountainside to find some shelter, when she noticed that the lightning had begun to behave in the most curious way. Instead of darting all over the place like ordinary lightning, it now all seemed to flash down at a place about two miles below her on the side of the mountain. And rather rapidly the flashes were coming nearer. Jane watched in amazement as the lightning jumped up the mountainside towards her. It was not until it struck a huge rock only twenty yards away, turning it instantly to dust and filling the air with a cloud of yellow smoke, that she realized the lightning might strike her. Turning round, she began to run as fast as she could up the little path.

The mountain was very steep and the wind now full in her face. Fast as she ran, Jane could hear the lightning gaining. Each time it struck, there was a noise like a bomb; and often it tore great chunks out of the mountainside and started little avalanches, which added their roar to the rumbling grumble of the thunder.

She was about to collapse and allow herself to be turned into a puff of yellow smoke ('it will be a million times worse than the worst electric shock,' she said to herself), when she saw ahead a glimmer of light coming from a long, thin crevice in the side of the mountain. She leapt towards it, and at the same time, with the most terrible CRASH, the lightning seemed to land right on top of her head.

It must, of course, have struck just behind her, because instead of an electric shock the force of the explosion hurled her into the air, luckily straight through the crevice. There was a moment's dizzy whirling and then Jane landed on something very soft.

It was a large bed. Sitting up, Jane saw that it stuck out from one side of a wide, ill-lit cave. Sitting in the middle on a stool was an elderly lady in a long black cloak. She smiled at Jane and said in a somewhat croaking voice, 'How very kind of you to come and keep an old lady company on a stormy night.'

'I'm Jane Charrington,' said Jane, crawling off the bed and coming across to shake hands, 'how do you do?'

The old lady held out a thin, bony hand, with very long, curved finger-nails, and smiled at her. 'How *you* do?' she croaked, 'I'm sure there is no need to tell you, but I am a witch. Please don't be alarmed.'

Looking quickly round, Jane saw that there was indeed no need to be told. Hanging on one wall were several long black cloaks, all with a pointed black hat, a broomstick and a fat black cat hanging beside them. From the ceiling dangled bunches of bats, and a great many string bags which Jane could see were full of skulls, herbs and odd-shaped lumps which were obviously pieces of newt, toad-stool, dried blood, etc. In front of the witch an enormous black cauldron gently bubbled over a log fire; by her side, as large as an Alsatian, crouched a huge toad, its skin glistening in the light of the candles.

'I'm very sorry to interrupt you,' said Jane, feeling rather timid despite the witch's assurances, 'but the lightning suddenly began to behave in a very odd manner.'

'I'm afraid that was my fault, my dear,' said the witch, 'I felt so much in need of company that I decided to tempt you here with the lightning. Please forgive me.'

'Oh, it's quite all right,' said Jane, 'I'm very glad. It's very nice here.' She still, however, felt rather nervous and turning round went and sat carefully on the edge of the bed again.

'Nice,' croaked the witch. 'but boring. So boring, boring, boring. Can you imagine what it's like being able to do exactly what you want? Soon you don't want anything. I long ago learnt everything a witch should know, except the one spell it seems impossible to discover, how to un-learn. Here I sit, year after year, producing storms and plagues and rainbows and everything else out of terrible boredom. All the time bored, bored, bored.'

'But can you do *anything*?' asked Jane.

'Anything,' said the witch, 'everything except stop being a witch. Would you like me to show you? Ask me.'

'Well, let me think,' said Jane, suddenly finding she could think of nothing at all. Then, seeing the gloomy gleaming eyes of the toad on her, she said, 'Could you turn your toad into a daffodil?'

'Certainly,' said the witch. She dipped one curved finger-nail into the cauldron, scattered some drops on the toad, muttered, and at once it blinked, quivered all over and then turned into a three-foot-high daffodil growing out of the rug.

'There you are,' croaked the witch. 'Quite simple. You may pick it if you wish.'

'Can you turn it back again?' asked Jane, feeling that it might be cruel to pick the toad-daffodil.

'Indeed I can,' said the witch, and muttering to herself she waved her bony fingers over the daffodil, which to Jane's pleasure immediately became a toad again. 'As a matter of fact it's quite useful,' the witch went on, leaning over and sniffing at the cauldron, 'this mixture is getting rather weak and could do with some toad. In you go.' The toad, however, did not move, but just squatted looking at the witch with an expression in its bulging eyes that Jane thought was unhappy. The witch looked at it crossly and pointed one curved finger-nail at the cauldron. '*In you go,*' she said sharply.

At this command, the toad gave a little sigh, looked sadly at Jane, and then sprang into the air and landed heavily in the cauldron, sinking at once out of sight.

'Oh, *poor* toad,' cried Jane, jumping off the bed and running to the cauldron, 'poor, poor toad. Please bring him back.'

'It's a painless death,' said the witch, 'the mixture acts as an instant anaesthetic and the heat cooks him in about eight seconds.'

'Oh but can't you bring him back?' said Jane.

'It's not a question of can or can't,' said the witch in a rather irritable voice, 'it's a question of having to keep on undoing things I've just done. I hate going backwards. However, I suppose I did offer to show you what I could do, so' – poking a long finger-nail into the steam hovering over the cauldron and then hooking it up as though pulling out a minnow on the end of a line – 'out you come,' she said in her commanding voice. And at once the toad floated up out of the cauldron and landed gently beside her chair again. He looked at Jane again; this time, she thought, with gratitude.

'Oh thank you,' said Jane, 'how clever you are.'

'Hardly clever,' croaked the witch, though she gave a pleased and crooked smile, 'I don't think it would be possible to imagine a simpler spell.'

'Could you just do one more thing?' said Jane hesitantly, 'one more tiny thing?'

'Very well,' said the witch, 'on one condition, I won't go backwards again.'

'I was wondering if you could just send him out onto the mountain to live happily ever afterwards,' said Jane.

'That doesn't require a spell at all,' said the witch, 'you seem so keen on him I thought you'd probably want him to become a Prince and me to send you both out onto the mountain to live happily ever afterwards. However, no doubt you are right. I'm obviously not going to get rid of him any other way. Off you go, toad.' At the wave of her hand, the toad didn't wait for an instant. With five huge rubbery jumps he covered the distance to the entrance, and with the sixth was gone.

The witch looked after him in silence, and then suddenly said, '*Happily* ever afterwards. He'll hardly be happy all alone. We need more toads.' She raised her arms, muttered rapidly to herself, and clapped her hands.

Immediately the cave was full of toads. Green toads,

grey toads, black toads, pink toads. Little toads and huge toads. Croaking, clacking, jumping, squelching, swelling, roaring, stinking toads; popping up from all over the place, and then at once bounding towards the end of the cave and out of it with their elastic legs stretched straight behind them. After five minutes when at least ten thousand toads, or so it seemed, had passed before Jane's amazed eyes, the witch clapped her hands and all was quiet again.

'You see,' she said, 'witches can be as kind and thoughtful as anyone else. It's only boredom makes us spiteful.'

'What shall we do now?' said Jane.

'Ah indeed!' said the witch, 'you see what I mean, once everything becomes possible, you don't want anything. After all, you can only want what you don't have, and now we have everything. We could talk, I suppose. Or you could talk and I could listen.'

There was a short pause, while Jane found she could think of nothing.

'Or I could talk,' said the witch, 'and you could listen. That, I confess, is the way round I prefer.'

'Or we could both talk and neither listen, or both listen and talk at the same time or taking it in turns,' said Jane. She suddenly felt rather reckless and bottled up. The witch looked at her with an odd expression.

'I think you need a sleep, my dear,' she said, 'however, for the moment I think I'll talk and you can listen.'

'It was interesting,' she began in a new, deep, monotonous voice which Jane felt could go on for ever, 'that the first spells you made me do were turning something into something else. People, when they first discover magic, always turn things into other things. Now . . .' and then the witch stopped. 'I know what we'll do,' she said briskly.

'What?' said Jane.

'We'll play the transformation game,' said the witch, 'I haven't played it for over a hundred years. It's very simple. The idea is that whatever your opponent turns into, you turn into something to beat it. For example, if I turned into a pin, you'd turn into a pin-cushion. If you turned into a fire, I'd turn into water, then you'd turn into a cow to drink me. I'd turn into a lion and so on. Now what would you do if I turned into butter?'

'Turn into a butter knife,' said Jane.

'Quite good,' said the witch. 'Of course you could have melted me. Right. Are you ready?'

'But I can't turn into anything,' said Jane. 'How do I do it?'

'Ah yes, very simple,' said the witch. She dipped a nail into the cauldron, scattered some drips over Jane and muttered to herself. 'Now all you have to do,' she said, 'is to think hard about what you'd like to be. You'll find that whatever it is, you will still be able to think and therefore turn yourself back. Of course, think is all you will be able to do which whatever you are can't. I mean, if I became soup, and you turned yourself into a spoon, you wouldn't be able to walk. You'd just be a thinking spoon. Unless, of course, you had turned yourself into a spoon with legs. Do you understand?'

'I think so,' said Jane.

'I should hope so,' said the witch. 'It is extremely simple. Now practise. Turn into something.'

Jane thought for a minute, and then found herself thinking of a box of matches. The next moment, there she was – squat, square, small and handy, a box of matches on the floor. In a very odd way, like having eaten a lot, she felt the matches inside her. From far above came the witch's voice; 'Well done,' it said, 'turn back.'

Because the witch had spoken, Jane thought of the witch. In an instant she was standing opposite and looking exactly like her, with long dark cloak, curved finger nails and pointed hat.

'No, *no*,' said the witch irritably, 'not into me. Turn into yourself.'

Jane thought hard about herself, and, after a confused moment when she felt herself turning into a mirror, returned with relief to her usual shape.

'Good,' said the witch. 'Very quick. Now, let us begin the transformation game. The rules are that if you can't think what to turn into after fifteen seconds, you lose ten points. I will begin.'

'Please start with something easy,' said Jane.

'Of course, I will,' answered a high voice at her feet. Looking down Jane saw a cat. That was certainly easy; she thought hard about dogs, and immediately shot down onto four furry legs and heard herself growling. But almost at once she felt something tighten round her neck; the witch had turned into a collar and lead. Leads reminded her of holding leads, so Jane imagined herself a hand and found she was holding the lead with all of her turned, as it were, into hand. The witch turned into warts. Quickly Jane thought herself a snail – Mrs Deal's cure for warts – and began to crawl over the hand. Then she felt something pecking at her, as the witch became a bird. Jane thought of her father's gun and at once felt herself seized. The witch had become a cowboy.

Jane became a sheriff. 'Well done,' said the cowboy, immediately becoming a troop of Indians, whooping and shouting. Jane, remembering an old film she'd seen on television, at once thought of a prairie fire. The witch became a rainstorm. And when the cave was half full of water, Jane first became a plug and then, feeling she was too small, a very large, thirsty cow. The witch turned into a lion. Jane a mouse. The witch a cat. Jane a dog. The witch a kennel. Jane an axe. The witch . . .

But at this moment Jane realized that the transformation could quite easily go on for ever. So when the witch turned into a grindstone and began spinning towards her, she decided to do nothing but just let the witch win.

After a moment the grindstone stopped spinning, and became the witch again. She waved her hands over the axe and made it Jane again. 'Ten points to me, I'm afraid,' she croaked with pleasure. 'Of course a grindstone is always difficult. As a matter of fact oil and water beat a grindstone, also a blacksmith and strangely enough, spit. If you'd become spit, I would then become a mouth, you could become a dentist or a gum shield, me the dentist's female assistant or a boxing glove, you . . .'

'Excuse me interrupting,' said Jane timidly, 'but though the grindstone was far too clever for me, I also remembered that I had a train to catch.'

'A train to catch?' said the witch 'well, you had certainly better go at once. Now, where was I? Yes – I'm a boxing glove or the dentist's assistant, you become a referee or a disease, I become a hospital or . . .'

'I really *must* go,' said Jane, 'thank you so much.' But the witch took no notice of her at all.

'. . . a hot water bottle or a toothmug,' she was saying, 'you would of course become a pin or a clumsy boy, I become a puncture outfit or a pin cushion or a cane.' Jane tip-toed to the door of the cave, then turned and waved goodbye. 'Thank you, witch,' she said under her breath in case the witch should hear and whisk her back. But there was no danger of that. The witch had her back to the door and was speaking as fast and as loudly as her croaking voice would allow.

'. . . I would become boredom or death or a railway time-table or a mattress,' she was shouting, 'you'd become possibility or a new-born baby or a cancellation or a house-on-fire. I . . .'

Very quickly and very quietly Jane stepped through the crevice and out onto the mountainside.

There was, however, no mountainside left. Nor, getting used to the sudden changes in Dream Land, was Jane particularly surprised. She found that she was standing in warm sunlight outside a small railway station. Hedges and fields stretched on every side and from the distance came the sound of church bells.

Walking up to the station, Jane went through the door marked 'booking office'. The hall was empty, though on it's far side, where an iron gate led to the platform, she could see the ticket collector asleep in his green ticket-collector's box. The little booking office window was open and just inside it someone had left an untidy heap of green tickets and a note saying 'Please take one'.

Jane did this and then walked over and prodded the ticket collector, whose spindly legs were blocking the way to the platform. At once he sprang to his feet, touched his cap and said, ' 'Oi be mighty zory Miss – oi do indeed. But a body git a mite dozzy these tiddly zummer arternoons.' Jane found she could scarcely understand what he said.

'What time is the next train and where is it going to?' she said briskly.

The ticket collector scratched his head, took a straw from his hair and put it in his mouth, then pulled a huge silver watch from his breast pocket, clicked it open, stared at it, clicked it shut, put the straw back in his hair and said, 'The zee-zide and market train do be due in foive minutes, miss.'

Somewhat impatient with this performance and still not certain what it meant, Jane let him punch several holes in her ticket, thanked him and hurried out onto the small platform. Neat notices on the other side showed that the station was called 'Job's Mill', and this curious name was also picked out in pansies on a little bank some way down the platform.

Jane did not have long to wait for the train. After a few minutes there came a gentle tooting and in a moment the engine appeared.

It was quite small, with a high funnel. Attached to the engine were four gaily painted carriages, which were quite bursting with people. Some sat on the roof, some clung to the doors or bulged out of windows; as the train came nearer many of them jumped down. And when the train actually stopped, snorting and steaming and blowing its whistle, it appeared to explode. Doors and windows were flung open and such a torrent of people poured out that Jane hurriedly climbed onto the little bank to avoid being squashed.

Jostling and pushing, they rushed past her. The men with hats, beards or side whiskers; the women with long sweeping skirts, bonnets and ringlets. All of them were carrying baskets of fruit, strings of onions, bundles of flapping chickens and every sort of thing from their farms. One giant of a man, with an apple-red face and knicker-bocker breeches, even had a calf flung across his broad shoulders.

The ticket collector tried for a moment to stem this crowd, Jane heard him cry 'Good gentle folk!', but then the man with the calf reached out and neatly tucked him under one huge arm and he was born away feebly shouting and waving his ticket puncher in the air. In a few minutes the station was quite empty.

Jane climbed thankfully into the last of the carriages and took a corner seat in one of the compartments. It was surprisingly tidy, with pretty curtains. Before long a man with a top hat came down the platform shutting doors, and a moment later the train started to move.

Jigadi-dig, jigadi-dig – the puffing of the engine was very peaceful as they slowly joggled through the pretty countryside. The sun had made the compartment almost too warm, and the soft seats covered in dark purple velvet were almost too comfortable. Jane began to feel sleepier and sleepier, and though she still remembered the Dream Master's stern warning about not sleeping, she couldn't remember if he had said anything about dozing. After all, she thought, she hadn't been to bed for two or three days, and though there was obviously something about Dream Land which made people need less sleep, they, or rather she, couldn't be expected to have no rest at all.

She was just about to stretch herself out on the seat, where she would no doubt have fallen at once into a deep and fatal sleep, when the train gave a loud whistle and stopped so suddenly that she was flung to the floor. At the same time, Jane heard the sound of shouts and cheering. She scrambled crossly to her feet and looked out of the window.

Just ahead was another little station, but this one was packed from end to end and on both platforms with a jumping, yelling crowd; all waving their arms, hats, shrimping nets and buckets and spades. The train moved slowly into it and stopped. At once all the people began to scramble in.

In seconds all the seats were taken. It made no difference, because they immediately began to sit on each other's knees. No one seemed to object. A huge woman stood in front of Jane, turned round, and then calmly sat down, completely enveloping her in petti-coats, knickers and skirts.

Jane began to struggle violently. But the woman, who was extremely heavy, paid not the slightest attention; and at last, nearly suffocating, Jane wriggled out from beneath her large legs and down onto the floor of the compartment.

Even here she was little better off. Everywhere was legs, with an occasional walking stick or spade; and as Jane crawled towards the door of the corridor these kicked and poked her and often prevented her progress altogether. But at last she reached the door, forced it open, and fell exhausted through it into the corridor, which for some reason was quite empty.

Almost at once the train started again and Jane, ignoring the hubbub from the compartments behind her, opened the window and looked out at the slowly passing scenery. It was very peaceful: little cottages, small square fields with white and brown cows in them and, once, a slow, sleepy river. Jane leant lower and lower out of the window, the warm air ruffling her hair, and was about to fall into a doze when she heard a loud splitting noise coming from the end of the corridor to her right.

She looked sharply round and saw that a large crack had appeared in the floor of the corridor. As she watched, it grew swiftly longer and wider, running up both sides and then beginning to travel across the curved ceiling.

'Stop!' cried Jane, 'look out!' But even as she shouted, the crack grew into a gap and with a splintering of wood and clang of metal the whole back of the train fell neatly away onto the track.

She looked wildly round for a communication cord, could not find one, and began to bang on the door of the compartment behind her. But as she did so, there came another splitting sound and a crack appeared at her very feet. Appeared, and at once began to grow. Jane turned and ran farther up the corridor. She stopped once to look back; but before she could do so a loud splitting noise at her heels sounded the appearance of another crack. The train was crumbling away under her feet.

She reached the next carriage, but had no time to stand and stare. Already the floor at her feet was falling away and bouncing onto the lines. Jane rushed up to the next carriage, and the next and the next. This was the last, and reaching its end she flung open the door and climbed up onto the roof by a ladder she found conveniently bolted to the side of the train. Then she jumped straight onto the coal at the back of the old-fashioned engine.

It was as well she did so, because when she looked back the last and final carriage had disappeared too.

The train was now moving very fast indeed. Jane climbed carefully down off the coal and into the engine driver's cabin. Perhaps, she thought, if I pull enough levers I may be able to stop it. But, before she could touch so much as a knob, she heard behind her a familiar and terrifying noise. It was the loud sound of tearing metal, followed by the rattle of coal falling onto the railway lines.

As quickly as she could, Jane pulled herself out of the little door at the side of the driver's cabin onto a narrow platform which ran beside the engine. Then, buffeted by the wind and nearly boiled by the boiler, she pulled herself forward, hearing behind her the crashes and clangs as the engine crumbled away.

At last she had reached the very front of the engine and was sitting in between the buffers. Her legs dangled over the railway lines as they shot underneath her. And behind her ... Jane looked back, and saw that behind her was nothing. Only the two front wheels of the train remained with Jane on top of them, and these now began to go slower and slower until eventually they stopped. And when they had done so, they simply faded quietly away, leaving Jane sitting comfortably on a wooden sleeper.

The front two wheels had stopped at the top of a low cliff which looked down onto a narrow shore of pebbles and endless grey sea. Quite close to where the line ended, Jane saw some steep white steps cut into the cliff side and a notice saying 'BEACH'. She hurried over to the steps and started down them.

'BEACH' was a rather exaggerated name for what she found at the bottom. The strip of pebbles was even narrower than it had looked from the top, and there was no sand at all. To her left, where the shore stretched quite straight until it reached the horizon, she could see nothing. And, though to her right it quite soon curved out of sight round the edge of the cliff, she felt that it was just as empty. The same was true of the sea. Flat and calm as a bowl of soup, it seemed to go on for ever, without waves or ships or sign of land, hardly licking the pebbles at its edge.

And yet Jane had a strange feeling that somehow she would cross it. Several times already in Dream Land she had felt she was on a special journey, and that was why she had felt no hesitation, for instance, about getting onto the train, and why the sudden appearance of the steps in the air, or the crevice leading to the witch's cave, had not surprised her. And so now she not only felt sure she must cross the sea, but was quite certain that some method or other would soon arrive to let her do so.

And indeed no sooner had she thought this than she heard a curious lolloping crunch coming from her right, and looking round saw a familiar figure bounding towards her. It was the witch's toad.

'I had to come and thank you,' panted the toad, landing heavily at her feet, 'for making the witch let me go.'

'Oh, not at all,' said Jane, 'I was very pleased to be able to do it. How are you?'

'Quite well, quite comfortable,' answered the toad in his rather deep voice, 'too many of us of course. It was a typically extravagant gesture; kindly meant no doubt, but far too extravagant.

'But how are *you*? Can I help in any way?'

'Well there is one thing,' said Jane, 'I very much want to get to the other side of this sea.'

'I think I can help,' said the toad, sounding pleased. 'I cannot take you all the way because it is too far. But I can certainly start you off. The water is delightfully warm.'

Jane waded out until the water came up to her waist. Then, on the toad's instructions, placed her arms tightly round his wrinkled neck and floated out behind him while with vigorous kicks of his long strong legs he started to swim through the water.

They swam for hours. At first the gentle sound of the sea washing past them, the soothing warmth of the water, filled Jane with the same longing to sleep she had felt on the train. But the toad, feeling her fingers loosen round his neck said, 'I shouldn't go to sleep, my dear,' and told her the story of his life with the witch. He had been with her a hundred years. ('A hundred years!' said Jane, 'and she was going to turn you into that spell mixture. How cruel!' 'A hundred years isn't much when you are thousands of years old like she is,' said the toad.) The story of his life was so interesting that she had no difficulty at all in listening; and she was still wide awake when, as evening fell, they swam to a small, bare rock poking up out of the grey sea.

'Here we are,' said the toad. 'Now, I am going to take you down quite deep into the sea to meet a new friend of mine. He will, I think, be able to help you further. But while we dive, I must ask you to hold your breath. It will take no more than a minute – but that is quite difficult.

'Ready?' said the toad.

Jane nodded nervously.

'One, two three – go!' cried the toad. And as she took an enormous breath, he stood on his head and with Jane clinging tightly to his neck plunged under the water.

Down, down, down, down – just as she was about to explode, Jane felt the toad shoot swiftly upwards, a dazzling light sparkled round her and a high, piercing voice said, 'Well, well, well – what a charming surprise!'

Panting, ears popping, Jane opened her eyes and saw—

But no. Perhaps it is best not to tell what she saw. To describe all Jane's adventures underneath and on top of that huge, grey and dangerous sea – to tell how she saw a man cut off his arm and roast it, how she was allowed to borrow a mermaid's tail, of the land of the giant but kindly jelly fish, of how she was captured and escaped from an atomic submarine – to tell all these and many others would take a book longer than this one is already. It is only possible to hurry on to her final adventure in Dream Land, the one which led to her escape, for that in the end is what became necessary, from that strange and mysterious place.

Jane's last adventure took place early one morning nearly three weeks after the toad had carried her to the rock. She was standing on the deck of a small pirate ship when all at once from out of the mist there came rushing the most enormous wave she had ever seen.

There was not even time to sound the alarm. With a terrible roar the wave crashed upon the ship, breaking it at once into hundreds of pieces. But Jane was caught by one of the whirlpools which all really large waves have spinning inside them, and in a moment was carried to the top. She was swept several miles until at last the wave crashed into a cliff, dumping Jane, wet and battered but unhurt in some soft bushes at its top.

She was near the entrance to a wide, grass road which soon disappeared over the top of a gentle slope. On either side as far as Jane could see, rose a forest of giant lilies.

The grass had obviously been recently mown, so Jane set off up the slope. She had not walked far, when she heard the tinkling of a great many little bells. Moments later, there appeared over the top of the hill a curious procession.

First came running about twenty young black boys in white cloaks and turbans, then twelve black boys carrying a large litter covered in orange and green cushions, finally more black boys.

When they reached Jane, they bowed low, the bells on their turbans tinkling, and pointed smiling to the litter. When she had climbed rather embarrassed into the cushions, they picked her up, turned round, and trotted away up the slope again.

From the top, Jane saw that the grass road first went down for a little way and then rose steeply up quite a high hill. And at the top of the hill, gleaming like sugar in the morning sunshine, was a large white palace. Big, onion-shaped lumps bulged all over its roof, two towers rose from its middle, and from all sides broad marble steps led down to the hundreds of fountains that surrounded it.

They soon reached the marble steps and ran up them. Then the little black boys lowered the litter, at the same time the two bronze doors in front of which they'd stopped slid silently open and there appeared a tall, white-robed man with a long, thin beard. He took two steps towards Jane, and bowed low.

'Welcome, brave girl,' he said, 'your travels and torments are over. Welcome to your just reward. This palace is yours. Here you will find rest and comfort, playmates and sweetmeats, plums and pomegranates, and sweet, sweet, sweet sleep.'

Jane stepped between the doors and saw stretching ahead a long, high, marble hall with pillars on either side. From invisible windows a dim light filtered through.

'I am your Vizier,' said the man, 'ask and it shall be done.'

'How do you mean this is mine?' said Jane, who already found the Vizier a little tiresome. 'Has someone given it to me? Who?'

'That I cannot yet say,' said the Vizier. 'All mysteries will be resolved later. Now we must refresh you,' and clapping his hands he beckoned a group of young black girls in white tunics and politely bowed Jane into their hands.

Jane, who was too tired even to think, went with them without protesting. All she wanted to do was to get back to Curl Castle and go to bed. She couldn't really understand why she hadn't gone days ago. In fact several times during the past three weeks she had been about to pull the piece of paper out of her jeans and quietly disappear only each time something like the huge wave or a particularly strange new monster had arrived to prevent her. These had also prevented her from dozing off, though she had often nearly done so. Now, however, she determined to return home as soon as she could; although she thought that first she might just find out a little more about the palace.

The young girls brought her to a chamber with a bath in it as big as a swimming pool. The moment she stepped into it Jane was thankful that she had waited at least till then.

The water in the pool was a deep purple, scented and warm. As she sat in it, Jane found her tiredness growing less and less, all the aches and bruises from her adventures were soothed away, and even her cuts closed up and healed before her eyes.

So relaxed did she feel, that when the little girls took away her jeans and her shirt and dressed her instead in a long pink silk dressing-gown, she did not call them back.

When she was ready, the girls lead her to the Vizier again, who bowed and said, 'Now Mistress, we have prepared a little entertainment for you. A few sweetmeats. Some music.' He clapped his hands and a dozen black boys appeared with an enormous black silk cushion the size of a sofa. When Jane had settled herself in it, they caught the tassels at its edge and carried her from the hall.

After a great many stairs, passages, corners, rooms and steps they arrived eventually at a small chamber which must have been nearly at the top of one of the tall towers. Through its wide, richly curtained windows Jane could see the forest of lilies stretching to the sparkling sea. The windows had no glass and, faint as a whisper, the delicate scent of the lilies was wafted in on a gentle breeze.

The chamber had thick carpets, tapestries on the walls and brightly coloured cushions everywhere. But in the middle of one wall a far larger heap of cushions formed a rough bed. Onto this the black boys carefully laid Jane and her giant cushion. All but four of them then left (backwards), and these four picked up guitars and very softly began to pluck them.

As soon as she heard the lovely notes, Jane felt a great drowsiness come over her. Snuggling down, she let herself relax deep into the cushions. As she had realized before, something about Dream Land made sleep less necessary, but even so she hadn't so much as dozed for three weeks. She sank deeper into the cushions, and heard at the same time the voice of the Vizier by her ear. 'You wish to sleep, Mistress? Then sleep, sleep, sleep.'

And then, as her eyes were closing, she seemed to hear another voice: '*If you are to return to your home you must never, never while you are here, fall asleep. Not for an instant, not for a single second however tired you are, however clever the temptations.*'

Immediately Jane pushed herself up and said in a loud voice, 'I will not go to sleep. Vizier.'

'Yes, Mistress?' said the Vizier bowing low.

'Stop that music,' said Jane, 'and bring me my jeans.'

'Your old clothes?' said the Vizier, waving his hands at the boys who at once stopped playing. 'Why do you want your old clothes? Have a sweetmeat. A pineapple?'

'I *want* my clothes, that's all,' said Jane. Suddenly she felt she was about to cry. 'I want my jeans.'

'Ah,' said the Vizier, 'you want the little message in the pocket?'

'Yes,' said Jane.

'But we have had it copied out for you on parchment,' said the Vizier. 'Bring the Mistress her parchment' he called, and immediately a black boy came running with a scroll in one hand.

Jane took it, unrolled it, read it. It was the spell! Without even bothering to say goodbye, she held it up and read in a slow, clear voice:

'Turn again, oh Book please turn,
  Now through your pages I return.'
Then shut her eyes.

Nothing happened. When she opened her eyes, she was still among the cushions. There was the Vizier, still bowing low. All that had changed was that one of the black boys had brought in a small, iron brazier, from which was rising a thin stream of pale blue smoke.

Jane said the words again, and then again. Still nothing happened. She leant back into the cushions and felt a hot tear run down her cheek. Very gently, the Vizier took the parchment from her hand. 'Do not worry, Mistress,' he said, 'do not cry. Just sleep.' As he spoke, the music began again, softly, soothingly.

And all at once, Jane didn't worry. After all, why not stay in this comfortable palace? She could make friends with the little black girls, go riding in the lily forest. She could sleep. Perhaps later she would find some way of returning.

But, as her eyes were closing, a curious thing happened. The scented blue smoke from the brazier, which was now drifting all over the room, suddenly reminded her of someone. It was of her father. It had the same smell as the stuff he put on his hair. And immediately, thinking of him, she remembered her mother, Mrs Deal,

Curl Castle. It seemed the most important thing in the world to go home.

With a great effort, she pushed herself up out of the cushions.

' I command you to get my clothes,' she said, 'at once.'

For a moment the Vizier looked coldly at her with his piercing black eyes. Then 'Very well,' he said, and turning round left the room.

He returned carrying her shirt and her jeans. Jane took them and eagerly searched the pockets. The paper was there. She opened it and, though the words were smudged by all the sea water, it had been tightly folded enough to protect them.

'Turn again, oh Book now turn,
  Back through your pages I return.'
said Jane.

And at once she felt herself sinking through the cushions and a great cloud seemed to sweep through the room.

She found herself sitting on the cover of the Book in the old library. Through the open windows came the sound of birds and the clinking of someone doing something in the garden.

Jane took off the pink dressing-gown and put on her jeans and shirt. Then she climbed the book shelves and hurried back to the lived-in part of the Castle.

At her bedroom she paused just long enough to write a note – 'PLEASE DO NOT WAKE SIGNED JANE' – pin it to her door, then undressed and slipped into bed. She fell asleep almost at once.

JANE was woken up, however, very much earlier than she had hoped. Mrs Deal, without any floods to distract her, had noticed her absence almost at once. At first she had not been very worried. It was understood that when Lord and Lady Charrington were away, Jane should always be allowed to go and stay with her friends, provided she told Mrs Deal first.

But after ten days, when no postcard or telephone message arrived, she decided to ring some of the friends up herself, taking the numbers from Lady Charrington's leather telephone book. As friend after friend said – no they *hadn't* seen Jane, Mrs Deal became more and more worried. She hurried into one of Lord Char-

rington's studies and dug out a large heap of his very old
private telephone books, some dating back to before the
First World War. Mrs Deal spent two days slowly tele-
phoning her way through them. Sometimes getting
rather odd replies, since many of the people in the books
had died or moved.

That very morning she had decided that if no message
arrived from Jane by lunch time, she would telegram
Lord and Lady Charrington in New York and call out
the police and the fire brigade. Her feelings when she
found Jane's note, therefore, were rather mixed. First
she felt relieved, then surprised and curious, and finally,
when she remembered her hours, in fact days, of tele-
phoning, she felt angry.

She hurried into the bedroom, pulled back the
curtains and then shook the little girl with a bony
hand.

'The death of me,' said Mrs Deal. 'You'll be the death
of me. Now where have you been, Lady Jane? You
know full well your mother said you must always tell me
when you go. I'll have a tale to tell her when she comes
home.'

Jane sat up blinking. She felt dizzy and had a head-
ache. 'I went to see some friends, Mrs Deal,' she said in
a small, I'm-sorry voice, 'I meant to write, but I was so
busy there wasn't time to let you know.' In a way this
was true.

'Friends indeed!' said Mrs Deal, 'I've telephoned all
your friends. I've telephoned all the friends the Earl and
Countess have ever had; and some of the old Earl's
friends' friends too. Now what have you been up to?'

Jane thought. It was no good telling Mrs Deal about

the Book. She wouldn't believe a word. 'She'd think I'm mad,' thought Jane.

'I've been staying with Kate, Sophie, Frances and Algy Behrens,' she said.

Now the Behrenses were the one family who didn't have a telephone. They lived in a boat on the Paddington Canal in London.

'I see,' said Mrs Deal. She patted her grey hair and made a vague dusting motion with her hand.

'Please, Mrs Deal,' said Jane, falling weakly back, 'I don't feel very well.' It was true. Not only was her head aching, but she felt very hot and rather sick.

And then Mrs Deal, who really loved Jane and was very pleased to see her back, and who in any case was now thinking it was very foolish of her to forget the Behrenses who had no telephone, Mrs Deal bent forward and gave her a soft dry kiss on the forehead.

'Well, never you mind,' she said, 'next time you send me a postcard or you'll have me grey before my time. Now just you lie there and we'll take your temperature.'

Jane's temperature was 102, so Mrs Deal called the doctor. He said that she had caught a feverish chill and must stay in bed. This she did for four days, sleeping most of the time, and having delicious invalid food like fish rolled up and cooked in milk, chicken broth and large white grapes from the Curl Castle greenhouses.

After a week she had completely recovered, except that Mrs Deal, although it was still what Jane considered summer, made her wrap up when she went outside.

She decided that she would not, for a while at least, go

inside the Book again. Partly because the last adventures, though she had enjoyed them, had been almost too exciting. And partly because Mrs Deal had told her that her father and mother were expected back in a fortnight. Jane longed to see them both again and was determined not to be roaming about somewhere in the Book when they returned; also she knew that, if she weren't at home when they arrived, it would be far harder to convince them that she'd been staying with the Behrenses than it had been Mrs Deal.

However, there were a lot of things to do at Curl. All the servants had their children back again, and Jane played with the ones she liked. The one she liked best was called Simon, the son of the head gardener, a boy about her own age with very black hair and dark brown eyes. Mrs Deal said he was 'a bundle of charms', and although Jane knew this to be untrue, since he sometimes teased her, fought her and made her cry, she much preferred playing with him to anyone else.

But one night, about a week after her return, and after a particularly long, hot day playing in the wood, Jane found she couldn't get to sleep. This was something which quite often happened to her. The night too was hot, with no wind, and even taking off her pyjamas and lying very still under just a sheet, always meant to make you cool, made no difference. She told herself stories, tried to think of nothing, even – completely useless – counted sheep.

When the clock in the stables struck twelve with deep, melodious chimes, she decided to go down to the kitchen and get herself a glass of milk and some fruit.

The Castle felt full of sleep when she stepped in her

dressing-gown out into the corridor. But even so, like all old houses, it gave continual creaks and made sudden noises as though the furniture, the walls and the floors were moving and stirring in the middle of strange dreams. Jane's bare feet made no sound on the thick carpets and her room was dimly lit by a faint moon shining through the windows.

When she reached the balcony running round the main hall (the same one Mrs Deal had been carried through by the piano during the flood), she stopped to look down. It was a little lighter here because of the many windows, and the chests and sofas threw shadows which, for a moment, Jane could imagine concealed monsters or burglars.

She was not on the whole a frightened girl, though anyone, whatever their age, can be frightened in the dark; but at that moment the ghosts of Curl Castle made her wish she was safe in bed again. It was true they normally stayed in their own separate bits – the little girl, for instance, around the old library, the monk in the bowling alley – and it was true that none of them had been seen for years. All the same, she looked closely round the moonlit hall and, especially after some particularly loud creaks, it was some time before she was quite sure nothing was there.

Through the hall, then into a short, uncarpeted stone passage, some steps, and finally another stone passage which led to the kitchen. It was while she was feeling her way down this that Jane suddenly heard a very definite loud noise. It was not a creak or a crack such as the sleeping furniture made but a clink; and almost at once it was repeated, as if someone, *or something* thought

Jane, had knocked a cup over in a saucer. A little far-ther, on tip-toe, and she saw that a dim, flickering light was coming from the kitchen door.

Jane crept gradually closer. Now she could hear dis-tinct sounds of careful movement. Her heart beating, she reached the door and slowly, slowly looked inside. What she saw for a moment stopped her breathing.

It was the little girl!

About Jane's size and wearing a long white dress, she was standing near the stove with a long candle in one hand. Her long dark hair was held back by a ribbon. With her other hand she was heaping various things onto a plate: an orange, some pieces of bread and, nearby, a glass of milk. It was seeing these, exactly the sort of thing she had planned to get for herself, that made Jane all at once feel quite unafraid. Perhaps, in fact, it wasn't *the* little girl at all, but just one of the servants' children dressed in a rather peculiar night-dress.

So stepping firmly into the doorway she said in a loud voice, 'What do you think you are doing here, please?'

At once the little girl gave a tremendous jump and knocked the orange onto the floor. Then turning round she ran and stood with her back to the sink, at the same time her appearance began to alter. Very slowly she became transparent. When Jane could see the draining board quite clearly through her stomach, the window-sill through her chest, and the taps through her right shoulder, the little girl raised her arms and said in a slow, ghostly voice, 'Wooo, wooo.'

'You don't frighten me,' said Jane, though she did

feel a bit nervous, and began to walk towards the sink.

'Wooooo, wooooo, *wooooo*,' went the little girl, pointing her small, transparent hands at Jane.

'You still don't frighten me,' said Jane, 'it's you who are frightened, otherwise you wouldn't go "woooo" like that,' and she continued to walk towards what, it was now obvious, was the ghost.

'Why aren't you frightened?' the little girl said, beginning to turn solid again. 'Nearly everyone else I've done that to has either fainted or else run away as fast as they could.'

'I'm just not,' said Jane, stopping by the table, 'but why do you do it? Do you want to frighten people?'

'Well, it stops them asking questions,' said the little girl, coming towards Jane. 'When I first came back here people would try and catch me and if I told them where I came from they didn't believe me. So I use the transparent trick which – well, which someone taught me.'

'Where *do* you come from, if you don't mind me asking?' said Jane.

'In a sort of way I come from a book,' said the little girl slowly.

'You mean the Book in the old library?' said Jane.

'Ah, you know about it?' answered the little girl. 'I wondered if it was you. I knew someone had found it by the footprints in the dust. But I must say I'm surprised to see you still here.'

'How do you mean?' said Jane.

'Oh, doesn't matter,' said the little girl, 'you'll find out.'

'But do you mean you *live* in the Book?' said Jane.

'Does that mean all the other people in it can come out and roam about Curl Castle?'

'Oh no,' said the little girl, 'but it's a long story; I can't explain now.'

Jane wondered if the little girl could answer any of her questions. She said, 'Well, why did you come here tonight?'

'Oh, all my friends have gone away for a week,' said the little girl. 'Also I was due to come. I hadn't realized it would be night.'

There was a small silence while Jane wondered what to say next, but found that she could only think of the questions the little girl wouldn't answer. Then suddenly the little girl said, 'You wouldn't like to come and stay with me, would you? We could have great fun and I could show you all my things. I might be able to teach you how to go transparent.'

Jane thought. There was Simon; then there were her mother and father, but they weren't coming back for a week. 'All right,' she said. But I can't stay more than six days.'

'Then let's go now,' said the little girl, 'if we're quick we'll just be in time for supper and then you can go to bed. I left about tea time.'

'First I must dress,' said Jane, 'and I *must* leave a note for Mrs Deal, or else she'll explode.'

They went upstairs together. Jane dressed rapidly in her jeans and a clean shirt and placed a sharp penknife in a back pocket. She wrote a quick note to Mrs Deal saying 'Gone to stay with Kate, Soph, Frances and Algy Behrens again. They may take me to Guernsey so don't bother to write. Back in six days. Love, Jane.' Then they set off through the long silent corridors for the old library.

During the walk, the little girl, whose name she discovered was Clarissa, didn't talk very much, so Jane told her about the great flood and how she'd blown open the tunnel.

'I remember that tunnel being dug,' said Clarissa.

'Do you?' said Jane, 'but surely that must have been hundreds of years ago – do you mean that . . .'

'Well, don't let's talk about it now,' said Clarissa, hastily interrupting her; 'we must hurry or it will be dark at home. Let's run.'

'Yes, all right,' said Jane, and they began to jog along, the candle flickering. She longed to ask Clarissa a great many questions. She was probably the only ghost she'd ever meet. If Clarissa *was* a ghost – she seemed far too solid.

Once they were both in the library, Clarissa put the candle, now burnt quite low, onto the chair and lifting open the Book slowly began to turn its pages.

Jane watched closely. She had noticed that each time she returned to the Book all the pictures had been different. So it had always seemed impossible to return to the same place again. After a while, she asked Clarissa about this.

'Well yes, the pictures do sort of change,' said Clarissa, 'but not as much as it seems. Once you've been in one place then somewhere in the Book there'll always be a bit of that place again. For instance, I think,' she stopped turning the pages and looked closely at the picture, 'yes, I recognize this part. It's not too far from my home. Now come and stand beside me and hold my hand. I'll say the words.'

With heart beating, Jane stepped up beside her and felt for her hand. At the same time she looked down to see where it was they were going. But before she could take in more than a general picture of paleness, which might have been water and might have been cloud, Clarissa had stepped off the Book and blown out the candle. 'It may come in useful,' she said, 'I'll leave the matches too.' Then she stepped back, took Jane's hand and said quietly:

'Shut eyes, do not look,
Close your pages on me Book.'

Once again, familiar now, Jane felt herself begin to sink down into the softening paper.

In the moonlit greyness of the old library, the heavy cover of the Book rose slowly up and without a sound closed firmly on the two little girls.

They were standing on the shores of what, until Clarissa told her it was a very large lake, Jane thought must be the sea. It was early evening, and in the fading light she could see that behind and stretching away on either side was a field of giant plants. Among the dense mass of forty-foot grasses, there were huge daisies and house-sized buttercups swaying in the wind. In the distance, skyscraper thistles and nettles rose still higher and even the crumbling grains of soil were, close-to, as large as Jane herself.

'Where are we?' she said.

'Quite near where I live,' said Clarissa; 'around here is a land of insects, but on the lake live the Lily people. But we must get home quickly. It's never very safe and even as late as this there's always a chance of hunter ants. But now look, try and get four pieces of grass about this long,' and she stretched her arms about two feet apart.

Jane found that the shorter blades of grass were no harder to cut than thick cardboard, and had soon sliced off four lengths with her penknife.

'You see, the lake is very salty,' said Clarissa, 'it's a salt lake, a sort of sea inside the land. This means it has a sort of skin on it like boiled milk. In some places you can even walk on it in shoes, but its better to have these pieces of grass.' She had meanwhile been tying the lengths of grass to both their feet with some leather straps she produced from her pocket. When they were both ready, she tucked her long dress up round her middle and then led the way to the edge of the lake.

Jane at once found out what she meant by a sort of skin. When she looked closely at the water, she could see it had a thick, almost oily appearance, and when she put a finger on the surface it dented down like pressing a sheet. If she pushed harder, the surface broke, but even then the water felt quite thick; her finger, when she pulled it out, tasted of salt and as it dried, little speckles of salt appeared on it.

'Now look,' said Clarissa, 'it's very easy. You sort of slide out on your grass, and then push one foot and then the other to move along. Like this.' Jane saw her walk carefully to the edge put one length of grass onto the surface and then push off with the other. In a moment she was gliding gracefully upon the top of the water, calling Jane to follow.

And it was in fact as easy as it looked. Jane found

that, nervous as she had been that she would simply sink straight to the bottom, her first foot was firmly supported. She pushed off with the second one and at once glided forward, rising with the heave of a long, gentle wave. To move forward she did just what she did when roller skating, which was shove with first one foot and then the other.

When Clarissa was sure Jane could do it, she said, 'Now we must go straight out for about half an hour. And don't worry if you fall over. It's impossible to sink and you'll just get wet and salty.'

They skated steadily in the direction of the setting sun. The thick yet slippery surface of the water moved slowly up and down in swelling waves and the speed gained sliding down into the valleys carried them almost up the other side so that a single push sent them over the crest. Unlike ordinary waves, these ones never broke or splashed.

Just as it was starting to grow really dark, Clarissa swooped closer to her and called out, 'Now we must go to the left a little. It's not far.' They turned left and after ten minutes, Clarissa called again. 'There you are. That's Lilytown.'

Peering ahead, Jane could just see numbers of small, black islands rising out of the sea. 'What are they?' she called. But Clarissa, obviously excited to be coming home again, had sped off to the right. Pushing hard with her feet, Jane raced after her.

Clarissa stopped at one of the islands. Jane swished up beside her, and found that it was not really an island at all. It was a vast lily leaf.

It was round and enormous, about the size of a tennis

court; its edge was turned up so that all round it ran a low wall. And in its middle, Jane could see the outline of a small cottage with a little shed standing near it.

'This is *my* lily leaf,' said Clarissa proudly, 'and that,' she pointed 'is my house. Now you must come in at once, you must be exhausted.'

They climbed easily over the rim of the leaf, took off their grass water-skis and walked up to the house. Jane felt the ground, or rather leaf, of the lily, sink a little at each step like walking on a firm, new mattress.

Clarissa's cottage had one large room downstairs, with a larder, and two small bedrooms and a bathroom upstairs. The downstairs room had comfortable arm-chairs round an iron cooking stove, a table, four little windows with gay curtains and had soft rush matting on the floor. While Jane looked around, Clarissa piled logs into the stove, lit several oil lamps and soon had every-thing warm and cheerful.

'It's lovely,' said Jane, 'it's so snug and sweet. I think it's lovely.'

'Yes, it is nice,' said Clarissa, 'but I'll show you round properly tomorrow.'

'Why are the chairs stuck to the floor?' asked Jane, who had tried to move one.

'Well, we sometimes have terrible storms,' said Clarissa, 'and then everything rocks and rocks and slides about. That's why my ornaments have to have little holes to sit in as well. But let's have some supper now and then go to bed.'

The two little girls prepared some bread, something like honey, some milk and some fruit, and when they had eaten it, excited and interested as she was, Jane found that she was in fact feeling very sleepy. After all, she told herself, it must be nearly four o'clock in the morning at Curl Castle. So Clarissa showed her to her room (which was very small, with a sloping ceiling, one window and a small bed covered in a blue and yellow eiderdown). They kissed each other goodnight, and in a few minutes she had fallen asleep.

Jane woke late, to find the sun streaming in through the little window. A cuckoo clock hanging opposite her showed it was already half past ten. And then, as she slowly stretched and yawned and thought about where she was, Jane noticed something rather strange. The whole room was gently rocking: the curtains, the oil lamp hanging from the ceiling, the dressing-gown on the back of the door which Clarissa had lent her, were all swinging together from side to side.

Jumping out of bed, Jane quickly dressed and ran down the stairs to the main room, staggering several times as the house lurched. Clarissa was already up and bustling about, and when she saw Jane, smiled happily.

'Did you sleep well?' she said. 'Have some breakfast then we'll go out. It's a lovely day.'

'Why is the house moving about?' said Jane, clinging tightly to the back of a chair. 'Is it a storm?'

'Oh no,' said Clarissa, 'It's often like this. There's a bit of a swell. But it's perfectly safe. The lily leaves have strong roots and never get swept away. Also the house is tightly pegged. You'd soon know if it was a real storm. I've been in some where it was almost like being upside down.'

Reassured, Jane sat down and had a delicious breakfast of hot milk, honey, and some rather curious eggs with very soft shells. Then, when she had washed and Clarissa had tied her own long hair back with a ribbon, the two girls went out onto the leaf.

It was indeed a lovely day. The sun shone bright and hot, a breeze blew towards the distant shore and all round them was the thick, oily sea, not sparkling, as at home, but gleaming in the sun. It was heaving in long, large swellings which were repeated, Jane saw, in long, large swellings moving across the green lily leaf at their feet. And behind them were the other lily leaves – Jane thought about two hundred. They all seemed much the same size as Clarissa's, and on each was a little house. Some had been joined together to hold larger houses. Floating everywhere between the leaves were large white blooms, themselves as big as cottages – the lily flowers.

Pointing excitedly, Clarissa showed Jane where her friends lived: 'That's Rupert's house, and that's Marius's,' she said, 'that's Sofka's and that's Inigo's and Aaron's and Luke's and Tino's, and that big house on two leaves is Petronella's shop. And you see that small, very pretty house there? That's Sophie Partridge's. Oh dear, if only you could have come earlier what fun we'd have had. You see all the Lily people go away at this time of the year for a long holiday.'

'I'd like to see it all, even if there's no one there,' said Jane, who longed to try sliding on the water again.

'Yes, all right,' said Clarissa, 'but first I must let Fly out.' And running over to the shed beside the house, she threw open its double doors.

To Jane's amazement there stepped slowly out, stop-

ping once or twice to rub its nose briskly with two long
and hairy front legs, the most enormous fly she had ever
seen.

'Out you come,' said Clarissa, in the sort of voice
Jane had heard girls use at pony club, 'steady now, mind
your wings.'

The fly was somewhat larger than a large horse. Its
body consisted of a series of overlapping, dark blue
plates and long hairs; on each side of its back two sets of
transparent wings were already quivering, and every
few seconds there shot from its jaws a tongue like a
thick tube, with a flat fleshy end. This made a loud
squelching noise as it hit the leaf. Clarissa looked fondly
at this monster for a moment, then stepping close she
gave it a friendly slap and said, 'Off you go, Fly.'

At once, with a whirring of wings, the giant fly shot
thirty feet into the air, hovered buzzing above them for a
moment, and then sped zig-zagging away in the direction of the shore.

'He's a bit surprising at first,' said Clarissa, laughing
at Jane's amazed expression, 'but you'll soon get used to
him. I'll take you for a ride when he gets back from
feeding. It's rather fun.'

Jane did not feel so sure of this, however she followed
Clarissa across the gently undulating lily and, when they
had both strapped on their grass skis, they climbed over
the rim and set off across the lake.

For nearly two hours Clarissa took her round Lilytown, telling her about the people and what she did
with them. About how the pale, honey-tasting nectar
came from the lily flowers, and how they had races on
the water beetles.

It was all very interesting, but what Jane enjoyed most was the skating or skiing. She found that the bigger the long, slow waves, the more fun it was. Soon, like Clarissa, she had learnt to wait for a large one, chase after it, and then balancing easily on its rounded top allow it to carry her swiftly forward. She practised swooping along the shallow troughs; practised turning, jumping, whizzing along on one leg. By lunch time, though exhausted, she felt quite sorry when Clarissa came up to her and said, 'I think we'd better go back. I left some spider's legs in the oven and we don't want them to spoil.'

The two girls had a good lunch (the spider's legs were rather tough, but Clarissa had made a delicious gravy to go with them) and then sat comfortably back in the soft chairs and ate some fudge.

It was very peaceful in the little cottage. The sun streamed in through the windows, the lily gently rocked, and a kettle gently steamed on the black stove. Jane felt that the moment had come to ask all the questions which Clarissa had not answered the day before; so she sat up and said in a careful voice: 'Clarissa, would you mind telling me about how you came here, and all about the Book and that sort of thing? You needn't if you don't want to,' she went on quickly, seeing Clarissa look rather worried and fidgety, 'but then I could tell you about my adventures.'

Clarissa thought for a moment. 'All right,' she said, 'I suppose you're sort of one of us. It's not that I mind telling, because it doesn't matter. It's just, well, I don't know . . .' she stopped. 'Well, it all began one winter when my mother and father had to go to London for the season, leaving me in Curl Castle with my brothers and sisters.' And settling back, she began to tell her story.

It was a very long story. It took three hours, because often Jane stopped her to ask questions, and because Clarissa, once started, told every single tiny thing that had happened.

Like Jane, Clarissa had found the Book because she was lonely. Her brothers and sisters had all been much older than she was, and in trying to find something to do, away from their loud, teasing games, she had accidentally stumbled across the old library. Like Jane she had found a piece of paper with the same strange words on it, and had at once begun to go adventuring.

Unlike Jane, however, she had discovered for herself quite quickly how to return to the same part of the Book, and this had made it much more fun. Because when she made friends she was always able to go back and see them again and have more adventures with them. Also in those days the servants as well as being very much more frightened of their masters and mistresses, always did what their masters' and mistresses' children told them, and Clarissa was able to do more or less what she liked. She began to spend weeks at a time in the Book. By the end of the winter, it seemed almost as unreal to return to Curl Castle as it had been at first to leave it.

Then, one day in the early spring, she had entered a land quite different from all the others she had been in before. From her description of it, Jane was at once certain that it was the Land of Dreams. She was about to say she had been there too, when for some reason she decided not to. And in a few moments it turned out this was very lucky. Clarissa had also seen the Dream Master, had liked him and still remembered his advice.

'He told me,' said Clarissa, 'that on no account was I to go to sleep. Well now, I know you haven't been there yet. But I know you will one day and that is the only reason I can tell you all this.'

'Yes,' said Jane in a vague voice, 'go on.'

'Well when he tells you about going to sleep,' said Clarissa, 'of course you can do what you like. But I can tell you it doesn't matter if you do go to sleep.' She looked rather anxiously at Jane, so Jane said brightly 'Oh, I'm sure I will go to sleep. I'm *always* going to sleep.' Clarissa smiled and went rapidly on. She too had found the grey sea, and she too, after many adventures, had ended up at the Palace surrounded by the forest of giant lilies. ('Perhaps that's why you like living on water lilies so much,' said Jane.) Like Jane she had been tempted and tempted with music and fans and slaves and incense and deep, soft, scented cushions. And suddenly she just couldn't be bothered any more and had, as she put it, sort of drifted off into a wonderful, long, endless sleep.

She had slept, she thought, for about 180 years. When she awoke she had been given a parchment with the Book's words and told politely she must go. So she had returned to Curl Castle, and of course it had quite changed. Her mother and father and all her brothers and sisters had long since died; and because the Castle looked very different and because people asked such irritating questions, she used to walk about transparent, a trick she had learnt on an earlier adventure. She also found that she was only able to return to Curl Castle three times a year. Though this made adventures in the Book much more dangerous, she had decided to live in the Book for ever. She had tried various places until at last she'd found the Land of the Lilies.

When she had finished, the two girls sat in silence for a while. Although Clarissa wasn't in the least unhappy, or even lonely, Jane felt sorry for her. It must be sad to have no mother or father or proper home.

'Look, Clarissa,' she said at last, 'would you like to come home with me? I know Mummy and Daddy would love you and we could play together and have adventures in the Book.'

'It's very very kind of you,' said Clarissa, 'but you see I don't really want to. It's all changed so much since I was there, and now this is my home. You wait till you have slept in the Palace for 180 years. You'll understand then.'

'But do you mean you'll never get married?' said Jane, 'never have children? Will you always be a little girl and never ever grow up?'

At once Clarissa sat up. 'I hate that word!' For the first time she looked upset, with an expression on her pretty face half angry and half frightened. 'Who wants to grow up anyway? Grown-ups die, they get tired, they're never excited; they don't understand. I want to be like this for ever and ever and ever.'

But though Clarissa looked defiantly ahead and spoke in a brave, loud voice, Jane saw two small tears, and then two more roll down her pink cheeks. She hurried over and put her arms round her.

'Don't cry, Clarissa,' she said, 'don't cry.'

'It's not that I'm sad,' said Clarissa, starting to smile, 'it's just that word. It always makes me cry without making me sad.'

'Tell me about the other people,' said Jane, 'the other non-Book people. Who are they?'

'Oh, mostly quite young,' said Clarissa, 'though there are one or two older ones. There's a very nice boy who writes poems. He says he can fly. But I don't often see them. You just sort of hear about them and sometimes see them.'

'But how do they get in,' said Jane, 'they can't all have Books. And they can't all use Curl Castle.'

'Oh they have maps,' said Clarissa vaguely, 'thoughts and mirrors and special walks. Some have books.' She didn't seem very interested, and kept on looking towards the windows, through which Jane could see the sky was already getting darker as evening began to fall.

Though she felt sorry for Clarissa, she also felt rather envious. In a way it would be nice not to go back to Curl Castle, or only go back when she wanted, when her parents were there.

'I suppose you're a sort of relation of mine,' she went on to Clarissa, 'are you a Charrington?'

'Yes,' said Clarissa.

Jane was beginning to work out what sort of relation, how many great-greats, etc, when Clarissa suddenly jumped out of her chair and ran to one of the windows. As she did so, the cottage which Jane had dimly noticed seemed to be swaying more than usual, gave a great lurch so that Clarissa was thrown quite roughly against the wall and Jane nearly fell out of her chair.

'I thought so,' said Clarissa, 'we're going to have a storm. They blow up in a moment at this time of the year. Here take this and come and help me.' She handed Jane an enormous spanner and together they hurried out onto the lily leaf.

It was very different from the sunny calm of the morning. A strong wind, blowing straight into their faces as they came from the cottage, was sweeping a cover of dark cloud low across the sky. Rising waves, which in some places had broken sluggishly over the rim of the lily, were beginning to lift them up and down, up and down, so that one moment they were hidden in a small, watery valley, and the next were on top of a rolling grey hill and able to look across the waters to where all the other lily houses were also bobbing up and down.

'Tighten all the bolts round the house,' shouted Clarissa above the wind. She pointed to a corner of the cottage and Jane saw that along the walls, where they rested on the leaf, large, six-sided bolts stuck up every two feet, holding it down. It was becoming difficult to stand, but by crawling on hands and knees she managed to pull the bolts as tight as she could with the large spanner.

When she had worked her way round to the front of the cottage again, she saw that Clarissa had opened the door of the shed and, clinging to it, was now anxiously scanning the sky. In one hand she held a long length of what looked like white, nylon rope; in the other a small wooden whistle which, when she blew it, gave a loud, piercing squeak.

As Jane pushed her way towards the shed, Clarissa

suddenly shouted, 'There he is!' and pointed excitedly into the air. Following her finger, Jane at last made out a tiny black object coming slowly towards them from the direction of the shore.

It was Fly. As they watched, though continually blown back and buffeted by the wind, he came gradually nearer. After about five minutes, he was hovering more or less above them.

Clarissa now stepped forward and with a quick movement threw the rope high into the air, holding fast to one end. Immediately, before it could be blown away by the wind, Fly plunged down and caught it nimbly in his mouth.

'Quick – help me!' shouted Clarissa. And as the rope tightened, Jane seized the end too, and they began to pull him in, hand over hand like pulling in a large kite. Soon he had landed and quickly they hustled him into his shed and closed the doors.

Now, on hands and knees, they struggled back to the cottage through what, even in the short time they had been out, had already turned into a real gale. Gigantic waves were beginning to break over the rim and the wind was making a curious and terrifying howling noise. But after five minutes they were safe inside and Clarissa was bolting and then double bolting the stout wooden doors.

Both girls were soaked to the skin from the water breaking across the leaf, and already the salt was making their clothes stiff and white.

'First we must change,' said Clarissa, 'and then make everything sort of ship-shape.'

Already it was impossible to stand without holding

on to something. Every few moments the floor became
first uphill and then downhill, and though the chairs and
tables were firmly pegged to the floor, cushions and
table-cloths slid off, and ornaments were falling out of
their holes.

When they had changed, Clarissa locked wooden
shutters over all the windows and lit storm lanterns.
Jane put all the ornaments in a special cupboard, which
had cotton-wool compartments, and coiled up the white
rope. ('It's really from one of the giant spiders on the
shore,' called Clarissa, 'very strong.') Before long the
little, rocking room was quite tidy, with everything that
could move carefully put away. The last thing Clarissa
did was to unpeg a bit of the rug in the middle of the
floor and roll it back. Jane saw that it covered a round
trap-door with sunk-in bolts. These Clarissa tightened
with a large box spanner.

'What's that?' Jane called.

'It leads to the lily stem,' Clarissa shouted back. 'I
was going to take you down but we'll have to wait till the
storm is over. It's rather exciting. It has steps going
round and round and leads right down to the bottom of
the lake where the roots are, and there are little bow
windows you can look out of. But it might be dangerous
just now, even though the stem is very strong and elastic
indeed.' Then holding onto the mantelpiece, a table and
the wall, she worked her way round until she could pull
herself into the chair next to Jane. 'What shall we talk
about?' she shouted.

So began one of the strangest nights Jane had ever
spent. Outside the storm raged louder and louder with a

fierce roaring noise. Every few moments the heaving, salty water crashed against the windows, and in the wind and buffeting the little house creaked and groaned like an old ship. It was almost impossible to hear each other speak. And in fact Jane had shouted back, 'What shall we *shout* about you mean,' though in fact she didn't want to talk or even think about anything at all.

It wasn't exactly that she felt sick. But often the lily almost stood on end and she had to cling to the chair to prevent herself falling out, and then the whole room would tilt up the other way, leaving her stomach quivering somewhere on the ceiling or so it felt. When this happened there came a deep thrumming from under the floor, which Clarissa explained was the lily stem vibrating as it stretched. And all the time the storm lanterns swung to and fro, so that mad shadows shot up and down the wall. Jane didn't quite feel sick, but she was glad that they had decided it was too rough to make any supper.

At about 10 o'clock they decided to go to bed. There was no sign of the storm ending, indeed the crashing and roaring and switch-backing seemed worse than ever, and even Clarissa, who was more used to it, was exhausted with clinging to her chair. So holding tight to banisters and door, they pulled themselves upstairs. Clarissa showed Jane how to strap herself into bed with the storm straps and then slithered out of the door and disappeared to her own room.

Although it was like being on a very soft, very violent see-saw, Jane almost immediately fell asleep.

WHEN she woke up in the morning, the storm was nearly over. The cottage still rocked, and there was still the sound of a high wind, but no longer the terrible tossing of the night, or the crash as heavy salt water thundered against the window panes.

Jane had woken once before at about two o'clock. She seemed to have heard some loud noise, like the twanging of a huge harp string or a deep bell; but after listening for a while she had decided it must have been the storm and had gone to sleep again.

She now lay warm and snug, watching the gentle swaying of the curtains and the sun coming through the cracks in the shutters. 'I wonder what they are doing at

Curl Castle,' she thought, and was just about to slip into a daydream about Mrs Deal and Simon and her mother and father, when the door flew open and Clarissa rushed in.

'Oh Jane,' she said, 'come quickly. The most terrible thing has happened. I don't know what we're going to do. Quickly, come downstairs,' and breathlessly she shot out of the room, 'I'm going to look for a gun,' she shouted back.

Jane pulled herself out of bed and scrambled into the clothes Clarissa had lent her the night before. What on earth could it be? A gun? Perhaps a dangerous crab had been swept onto the leaf by the storm and was about to attack them.

When she came downstairs she found Clarissa kneeling by one of the cupboards holding an old flint-lock gun in her hands. 'It's old, but I think it still fires,' she said, as Jane came in.

'But what's happened?' said Jane, 'what is it? Are we in deadly danger?'

'Look,' said Clarissa. She went to the door and Jane followed her out onto the leaf. It was a lovely sunny day, with a brisk breeze. The leaf was dry again though covered with bits of wood and weed. But this was not what Clarissa was pointing at so dramatically. Following her finger, Jane looked. And at once she realized. *The leaf had moved*.

Gone were the other lilies. Gone the distant shore. Instead, they were in a wide passage between two islands, or in an enormous river. The current was very fast, carrying them between the steep mountains which rose up on either side.

'You see?' said Clarissa, 'the storm must have broken the lily stem.'

'Yes, and I think I heard it,' said Jane.

'Did you?' said Clarissa. 'But do you realize where it has swept us? To where the ants live. At least I think so.'

'Ants?' said Jane. 'Why does that matter?'

'Come and have breakfast,' said Clarissa, 'and I'll explain. But we must keep a watch on the shore.'

While they prepared a large and delicious breakfast of soft-shelled beetle eggs, lily honey and toast, and while they ate it, she told Jane about the ants.

They were supposed to live in giant ant heaps at the far end of the lake. 'Supposed to', because none of the Lily folk now alive had ever ventured there; but there were stories of earlier expeditions which had set out to explore and never returned. The ants were hunters who lived entirely off flesh, and during the day they sped in their millions through the tall grasses of the lake shore killing and eating. One thing about them was unusual. They never hunted at night. Indeed they were supposed to go into a sort of trance as soon as the sun fell and not come out of it again till sunrise. If you were captured, Clarissa said, this was the only time you could escape; provided you were still alive, or not had a leg or two snipped off.

'But are you sure this is the right end of the lake?' asked Jane.

'Not really,' said Clarissa, 'but the storm blew from the west and the ants are said to live in the east.'

'Anyway,' said Jane, 'this river or passage has very

wide-apart banks. Perhaps we'll never get nearer to them.'

It was true that the banks were far away; nearly a mile on either side. And they remained at this comforting distance all the morning as the two girls worked on the cottage. First they cleared away all the weed and debris from the storm. They also tied a plank to the back of the leaf with some spider-web rope, so that they could steer the leaf well away from the banks and give the ants no chance to spring aboard.

Throughout the morning they had both kept looking at the banks and both had agreed they were as far apart as ever. Gradually, however, though she still said this, Jane felt that somehow they were not as far apart as before. Inch by inch they seemed to be closing in. Then she would look again, and they did in fact look just as far away.

But now there could be no doubt about it. They were nearer. She could see tall grasses instead of a blur and rocks stood out clearly.

'Clarissa,' said Jane, standing up, 'the awful thing is – I mean I think the awful thing is . . .' She pointed out of the window.

'I know,' said Clarissa, 'I thought so too, but I didn't like to say anything.'

They ran out onto the leaf and what they saw was even more alarming. The river, or passage, had begun to twist. They were at that moment swinging round a long left bend and the lily, as a result, was being slowly swept towards the right-hand bank. They seized the plank and managed to steer gradually back to the middle again.

Once round the corner, they saw ahead another bend, and then another. Each time they had to strain on the plank to force the lily back into the centre. Each time, though it was difficult to be sure, the banks seemed a little closer.

It was after about ten bends that they passed a little clearing in the tall grasses on the left. Jane was staring idly at this when all at once the grasses parted and a huge insect ran swiftly across the space. As large as a horse, it had six legs, long, low-hanging jaws, bulging black eyes and two bodies joined like a wasp.

'Look, Clarissa,' she shouted. But it had gone. The next instant another appeared. And then five more. At least thirty had crossed the clearing by the time it had slipped out of sight behind them.

'The ants,' whispered Clarissa. 'Oh Jane, whatever are we to do?'

Soon they realized that they were surrounded by ants. The banks were now not more than fifty yards apart and drawing closer. Having seen the ants once, they could more easily see them again. A flash of fierce dark eyes staring motionless out of the grass; a sudden swirl of stems as the large bodies brushed through them; a glimpse of a shiny back catching the sun. The ants were quite silent, easily keeping up with the swiftly flowing current and the little cottage.

Or rather the once swiftly flowing current. Because Jane now noticed that quite suddenly the current had begun to slow down. The lily became harder and harder to steer. Soon the waters stopped moving altogether and then, sluggishly, the lily began very gently to drift towards the left-hand bank, spinning as it drifted.

'What shall we *do*?' said Clarissa for the second time. 'We'll be eaten alive.'

'We must escape at once,' said Jane. 'Will Fly carry two?'

'I think so,' said Clarissa, 'Yes, I'm sure he will for a little way. He's very strong.'

'Quick then,' said Jane, 'we've only a few minutes. You get Fly.'

As Clarissa unbarred the hut and began to coax the startled fly out onto the leaf, Jane dashed into the cottage and fetched the spider's-web rope from the wall. Then she hurried out and joined Clarissa.

The fly was now standing quietly, though Jane could see that its stubby transparent wings were quivering in the sunlight. Clarissa helped her up onto its broad back, and was just holding out a hand to be pulled up herself, when she suddenly said, 'I must just get the gun,' and rushed off into the cottage.

The lily had now drifted to within ten feet of the shore, where it seemed for the moment to have stopped. But everything the girls had done had been watched intently by hundreds of hungry eyes along the bank. And gradually there could just be heard a very high, sinister whistling, more like a vibration than a noise. And now, suddenly, Jane saw the grass swish aside. For an instant she saw one of the huge insects gathered back on its six hairy legs. Then it sprang out over the water towards the lily.

There was a fearful lurch as its forelegs crashed onto the leaf. It nearly slipped off, but then digging into the soft fibre with the cruel pincers which were its feet, it pulled itself dripping out of the water. The fly, with Jane

clinging to it, backed trembling away. At the same time
Clarissa came running from the cottage with her gun.

She saw the ant. Screamed. Fired a wild shot, which
missed by many feet, and then, as she turned to run to
Jane, was seized and lifted from the ground by one snap
of the long jaws.

'Help, Jane! Help!' she cried.

But Jane could do nothing. The fly had been terrified
at the appearance of the ant. At the sound of the gun it
had become uncontrollable. With a leap and a whirring
of its powerful wings it had shot into the air, and now
Jane stared down in agony a hundred feet above the
terrible scene below.

She saw Clarissa struggling, heard her call. Saw the
ant shake its head and fix her more firmly between its
jaws. Then watched while it sprang off the leaf, land
some way out in the water, swim to shore and disappear
into the darkness of the tall, waving grasses.

'Don't worry, Clarissa,' she shouted down as loudly
as she could, 'I'll rescue you.' There came no answering
shout.

It took Jane some time to learn how to control the fly.
The sections on its back were covered in coarse, short
hairs, which made sitting quite comfortable and hold-
ing-on easy. After several experiments such as saying
'Go *down*, Fly, *down*,' she found that all she needed to
do was to pull the hair on its left to make it go left, on
the right to make it go right, to pull the hair on the
middle of its back to make it go up, and push down to
make it go down. Soon she was skimming just above the
feathery tops of the grasses more or less where she had
seen Clarissa disappear.

For a long time she saw nothing. The grass forest seemed deserted, even the smallest insects having been devoured by the hordes of hunter ants. But suddenly she saw some way ahead, as she flew back along the shore, a waving movement in the grass. She forced Fly lower, till the grass tops brushed his legs, and saw, now here, now there, the unmistakable forms of giant ants rushing along below.

It was a long line, which must have held some two thousand ants, and Jane raced back and forth from end to end of it. Once or twice she thought she caught a glimpse of an ant with something white in its mouth, but she couldn't be sure.

It had been about the middle of the afternoon when the ant had attacked. It was getting on for early evening when Jane noticed that the line of ants had turned away from the shore and begun to climb up towards the mountains. Before long she saw ahead a wide clearing, filled with large tea-cosy shaped hillocks nearly as high as the grass. The clearing, and the surface of the hillocks were swarming with ants and she could hear the same sinister whistling she had heard before. Soon the line of ants entered the clearing and poured in a black stream towards the nearest hillock. In a few minutes they had all disappeared inside it.

Jane at once decided what she had to do. First, return to the lily and rest Fly. He had now been in the air for some two hours and was obviously getting tired. Then she would get some equipment and return to rescue Clarissa.

She therefore fixed the position of the clearing firmly

in her mind (luckily it was on a line between two mountain peaks on either side of the river), then, pulling Fly's hair, turned him round and headed back the way she had come.

For half an hour they flew down above the waving tops of the grass jungle. The unpleasant whistling soon died away behind them and the only sound was the gentle humming of the fly's wings and the swish of air past Jane's ears. Gradually, as they drew closer, the strip of water grew wider and wider, glinting in the evening sun. They were directly above it, and Jane was about to turn Fly left in search of the lily, when she saw to her surprise that it was already there, floating on the water below her. She pressed Fly's back and they plummeted down.

Fly was quite wobbly with exhaustion and Jane quickly bundled him into his hut, where she was interested to see him instantly shoot out his long tongue and begin to suck greedily from a bucket in the corner. Then she hurried out and, carefully avoiding the ugly gash which the ant had left with its pincers, ran into the cottage to fetch the emergency anchor that Clarissa had shown her hanging in one of the cupboards. She found it, attached its rope to the peg and threw it overboard. A moment later she felt a comforting jerk as it caught on the bottom. For some reason the current in the river was flowing in the opposite direction, carrying the lily back to the lake. Now, firmly anchored, she would only have to fly straight up the mountainside again to return to the clearing. Jane hurried back into the cottage again.

First she collected a bag of things for Clarissa:

bandages, some ointment, and a bottle of lily milk. Then a bag of things for the rescue: thirty-six reels of white cotton, which she found in the store room, some matches, her penknife, and a hurricane lamp full of oil. She also put into her pocket the wooden whistle with which Clarissa had called Fly in the storm. Next she had a quick meal and washed her face and hands to refresh herself.

Fly also looked much better when she carried all the things out to his hut. He trembled his wings at her in a way she decided was affectionate, and didn't seem to mind in the least when she tied all her bundles into the thick hair on his back.

It took them half an hour of straight flying to reach the clearing again. As Jane brought the fly quietly in to land on the branches of one of the bushes at the edge, the sun finally went down behind the mountains and darkness fell.

The first thing Jane noticed, was the silence. The whistling had stopped. Nor, as her eyes grew used to the darkness, could she see any movement which might have been an ant. But this did not mean very much. They could easily just be asleep. Clarissa had said they were only supposed to go into a trance at night. Jane knew that she would only find out if this were true when she actually tried to enter the ant hill itself. But before doing this she decided to wait until she was quite sure there were no ants and until the moon rose to give light.

She waited on the branch for several hours. Eventually, at about half past twelve, a large moon rose high into the sky above her head. The huge hillocks cast long black shadows and in a ghostly way it seemed almost as light as day.

Jane decided she could put it off no longer. She crept back along the branch and up onto Fly's back. Then tugging gently she urged him into the air and they soared out, hovered for a moment and then came lightly down onto the ant hill nearest the riverside edge of the clearing.

Its top was quite broad, made of dried earth and long stalks of dead grass. To one of these she tied Fly with a thin piece of spider's rope. Not to stop him escaping if, say, an ant attacked him, but because she hoped that it would keep him there till she came back. *If* she came back.

She took the two bags and slung them over her shoulder, lit the hurricane lamp and with a last longing look down at the empty, silent, moon-lit clearing, walked slowly towards a large black hole in the centre of the hill top.

Holding up the lamp, she could see that the hole led very gradually down into the hill. An unpleasant, warm breeze, smelling slightly of rotten meat came from it; but that was all. No sound. Nothing to see.

Slowly, heart beating, she took a few steps, then stopped to listen. A few more steps. Another stop. And now, already out of sight of the entrance, the tunnel forked. Putting down the lamp, Jane took the first of her reels of cotton, tied one end firmly to a stick of grass and then started walking slowly on again, unreeling the cotton behind her.

The tunnel slope became steeper, the smell of rotten meat stronger, and now the divisions, forks and side turnings became more and more numerous. Jane had just taken a left turn and was holding her lantern high above her head, when she saw her first ant.

It was standing ten feet away, leaning against the side of the tunnel and staring at her fiercely, its large, black eyes glinting in the light.

Yet it did not move. And as she came slowly closer, clutching her penknife, it was plain that it had no interest in her at all. Even when she was right under its huge, hideous jaws, and reached out a hand to poke one of its hairy legs, it remained quite still. Jane's lamp hissed in the silence.

At once she felt better. So it was true about the trance. Now, it was safe to search for Clarissa as fast as she could; safe, that is, till dawn. Taking out another cotton reel, she hurried rapidly on.

As she drew near the centre of the ant hill, the tunnels became more like hundreds of huge rooms joined together. In some she found giant ant eggs, lying row upon row guarded by sleeping ants. In others were whole jumbles of ants, in black motionless piles. And in some, the most disgusting, were heaps of dead grass-hoppers, flies and moths. It was these that smelt so strongly, but though it revolted her Jane always looked carefully into them, terrified of finding the body of her friend.

But of Clarissa there was no sign. And slowly Jane began to despair. Perhaps she had already been eaten alive. Or perhaps she had already struggled free, taking, like Jane, advantage of the ants' trance and was even now running through the grasses to the river. And how, Jane wondered, could she ever find anything in this vast heap? She had now been searching for several hours. The tunnels and rooms became more and more confusing. Several times she found herself in places which already had cotton along their walls and had to wind herself back to save thread. And in fact the cotton reels were beginning to run low. She longed to escape from the hot, dark walls, the army of motionless, frightening ants, the smell.

It was at this moment that she found her first real clue that Clarissa was, or had been, in the ant hill. She was stumbling down yet another dark, uneven tunnel, when her foot kicked against something. Looking down, she saw Clarissa's gun lying by the wall. She picked it up excitedly. It seemed very unlikely that an ant would have brought it back without Clarissa; but quite possible that Clarissa would have clung to it for as long as she could.

Now Jane began to search harder than ever. She looked into every crevice, every little room and tunnel, always, when she had gone some way from the gun, returning to it and setting out in a new direction. Even so she nearly missed Clarissa.

She had searched a large chamber in which all the ants had tumbled over, and was just about to leave it, when she noticed in the farthest corner one huge ant still upright. It was frozen in a guarding position. She clambered towards it, and coming close held her lamp high. There, lying between the thick hairy legs, was Clarissa's body.

She was bound to the neck in tight strands of what seemed like nylon. Her face was white, her eyes closed, but putting her cheek very close, Jane could feel a faint breath. She was alive! Swiftly Jane took out a penknife and cut through the white strands. As they fell away, she saw that poor Clarissa's arms and legs were all blue and swollen and felt very cold. But at once she began to massage them and move them about.

After about five minutes, Clarissa gave a low moan. Then, as Jane continued to massage, she heard her murmur, 'Where am I? What is it? Oh my arms, my legs.'

'It's me,' said Jane, 'Jane.' Clarissa's eyes opened, then shut, then opened and fixed on Jane. 'Jane,' she said weakly.

At once Jane lifted up her head and shoulders and propped them against her chest. Then she took the bottle of lily milk out of the bag and put it to Clarissa's mouth. 'You must drink this,' she said.

A lot was spilt, but soon Clarissa was drinking it hungrily, in huge gulps. Then Jane began to massage her again, bending the numb legs and rubbing the cold arms. At last, 'Now try and stand,' she said.

'I can't,' said Clarissa.

'You must,' said Jane. 'We've got to escape.' Very slowly, she dragged Clarissa to her feet, held her swaying, while Clarissa weakly tried to move her legs.

And then, faint and terrifying, they heard a noise. It was a high, wavering, piercing whistle, a vibration which seemed to come from the very heart of the ant hill. The ants were waking up.

Immediately Jane dragged Clarissa to the entrance of the chamber and out into the tunnel.

'Please, Clarissa,' she said urgently, 'please try and walk.'

'I am trying,' said Clarissa. 'I am, I am.' She was so weak that Jane realized it would be impossible to follow the cotton back up to the top of the ant hill. They would have to go down, and even that was hard enough. At every step Clarissa's legs gave way and Jane really had to carry her.

Now she could hear and feel the ant hill coming alive all round them. The whistling spread from room to room, down the winding tunnels, seeming to penetrate the walls themselves. And as they stumbled down, the hurricane lamp sending its swaying light ahead, Jane could see movements in the chambers on either side of them. Ants stretching, ants standing up and clashing their jaws, ants getting ready for another day's hunting.

She felt herself tiring. Twice Clarissa fell down and had to be dragged to her feet again. Jane was beginning to feel that they would never escape, that any minute an ant would spring out and seize them, when suddenly she saw a gleam of light ahead. Another three stumbling steps and there in front of them was a wide entrance.

'Quick Clarissa,' she said, 'look, we can escape. Quick.' With a last effort she heaved her friend along, Clarissa's legs managed a few more steps, and the next moment they were out in the early morning sun, blinking in front of the ant hill.

But still not safe. All round them stretched the bare earth, the air was filled with a whistling that was now deafening, and as Jane watched an ant ran from the entrance of a nearby hill, seemed to sniff the air and then ran back. It was at this moment that Clarissa began to sink to her knees. 'I can't go on,' she whispered. 'Jane, say the words of the Book and escape. Leave me behind.'

And suddenly Jane remembered Fly. As Clarissa lay fainting at her feet, Jane began to rummage frenziedly in one of the bags. In a moment she had found the whistle, in a moment blown it, and then blown it again and again.

Could he hear above the ants? Would he break the grass? Jane blew again. And then, looking up, she saw the fly hovering high above them. She waved. Blew the whistle. Fly saw her, buzzed down, hesitated, buzzed down farther, and eventually landed lightly beside them. Jane dragged Clarissa across the ground and somehow pushed and heaved her onto his back. Then she scrambled up herself, pulled at the stiff hairs, and very slowly they began to rise into the air.

Below them an ant dashed out of the ant hill. Stood looking left and right, and then dashed back.

There is really very little more to tell. They flew by easy stages back to the lily leaf and Jane, after putting oint-ment on Clarissa's bruises and washing the worst of the earth off her, put her straight to bed. Then she had a bath and went to bed herself.

She slept all that day and the following night, waking the next morning completely refreshed but very hungry. Clarissa too, though still stiff and bruised, was well enough to get up and together they made an enormous breakfast. Then, Clarissa doing the easy things, they began to tidy the cottage.

Jane stayed two more days. They mended the rip in the leaf, went for rides on Fly, and making a sail out of some sheets started to get the lily back to Lilytown. But at the end of the second day Jane decided that the time had come to return to Curl Castle. She had now been away six nights and she didn't want to get back after her father and mother.

Clarissa was miserable when she heard. 'Oh *please* don't go,' she said, 'please. You've saved my life and we have had such fun. I want you to meet my friends and come down the lily stem and go fishing and show you how to become transparent. Please stay, please, please, *please*.'

But Jane explained that, though she'd love to, she simply had to get back.

'But its not like going away for *ever*,' she said. 'You come and see me next time you're due to come through the Book and I'll come and see you again *very* soon.'

'And anyway soon you'll go into the long sleep and then in the end we can be together for ever,' said Clarissa. But Jane pretended not to hear this and hurried into the cottage to get her jeans and her shirt and have a last look round.

Because in fact she too was sorry to go. She loved the little house, with its curtains and sweet furniture; and she had grown fond of Fly; but most of all she loved Clarissa, with her dark hair and the gay way she liked doing things. And yet at the same time there was something sad about her, something that worried Jane and made her want to protect her.

When she came out onto the leaf she put her arms round her and kissed her. 'Goodbye,' she said, 'goodbye.' And then seeing that Clarissa was unable to speak, but could only brush two large tears away from her eyes, she squeezed her very tightly and said, 'Don't worry, I'll come again soon. I'll see you *very* soon. I promise. Goodbye.'

'Goodbye Jane,' whispered Clarissa, 'goodbye.'

And very quickly Jane said the words of the Book, because she knew that otherwise she'd cry too.

10. THE END OF
LORD AND LADY CHARRINGTON

IT WAS pitch dark when Jane stepped out of the Book in the old library. However she soon found the matches and candle which Clarissa had left on the chair, and, having lit them, quickly climbed up the shelves and down the iron pegs on the other side.

Once she had reached the bedroom she wrote a note for Mrs Deal – 'Have got back, love Jane' – brushed her teeth and climbed into bed. In a moment she was asleep.

She was woken by the familiar bony hands and Mrs Deal's voice at its most brisk. 'So the wanderer returns! Whatever next! Now up you get and have a good wash and then down to your father and mother. They arrived back late last night. But don't you worry. I said you were with the Behrenses and would be back this morning, keeping my fingers crossed.'

Jane leapt out of bed, pulled on her dressing gown and raced out of the room. Mummy and Daddy! She threw open their door and with a great leap sprang into the middle of the big, pink bed.

'Mummy!' she cried.

'Darling!' cried Lady Charrington, holding out her long arms.

'Well, well,' said Lord Charrington, putting down his newspaper, and taking off his glasses and then putting them on again. He put his big arms round her and pulled her against his silk pyjamas.

What had she been doing? How were the Behrenses ('very well' said Jane); did she know that their friend Sabrina had had a baby boy and was going to call it Benjamin, so nice for Jenny to have a brother . . . nestling between their pillows Jane talked and listened for half an hour. Then she said, 'And what was America like? Was it fabulous?'

At this there came a little silence. Or rather her mother became silent. Her father began to smile and make little chuffing noises which Jane knew meant he was about to say something interesting and, to him, exciting.

'Your father has something to tell you,' said Lady Charrington in a mournful voice.

'Yes,' said her father, 'yes. Now, Jane dear, in America they lead a very different sort of life to the one we lead here.'

Lord Charrington had been extremely impressed by America. He had been a great many times before, but somehow this time had been different. Although he was an Earl, for the first time they treated him as though he weren't one. And he had found that this meant they treated him exactly as they had treated him before. This is not as complicated as it sounds. It happened because in an hotel one day he gave his name by mistake as Mr Charrington instead of Lord Charrington, and yet they still said 'This way, sir' and treated him with all the respect he was used to. Although the fact that he was obviously very rich may have had something to do with it, this had impressed Lord Charrington. After that he had called himself Mr Charrington all over the place. And still they had treated him with respect. Lord Charrington had decided that it was the respect due to him as a HUMAN BEING. As well as this he had read certain books which had impressed him; the result was that Lord Charrington had decided to drop his title and be known, as soon as certain papers had been signed in London, as Mr Charrington. It was this that he tried to explain to Jane as shortly as he could.

'And I have decided we shall live as ordinary people as well,' he said, one arm round his daughter, the other waving in front of them. 'We shall give up this huge castle and live in an ordinary council house by the sea.' He made a little shape like a box in the air. 'I have already ordered one at Aldeburgh in Suffolk in the name of Mr and Mrs Charrington. I shall keep the Observatory of course. That will be my job. I shall be Mr Charrington the Scientist. The rest of the Castle I have been dividing up: the middle is for the National Trust, the South Wing is for a Mental Hospital, the East Wing is for an Old People's Home, the West Wing is to be a Youth Hostel and the North Wing is going to be a Holiday Camp. The roof will be bowling alleys, skating rinks, dance floors and swimming pools. Now, what do you think of it?'

Jane found she could think of nothing at all. 'Can I take all my things to the council house?' she said.

'We may all take anything we like,' said Lord Charrington, 'your mother has – ahem – already begun to make a little list.'

'When do we go?' said Jane.

'As soon as possible,' said Lord Charrington, 'next week.'

At this, Lady Charrington gave a low moan. Seeing that she looked rather sad, Jane put her arms round her.

'Oh, poor Mummy,' she said, 'don't you want to move?'

'Your father knows best,' said Lady Charrington. But she gave a little sigh. She *enjoyed* being a Countess. She liked being called M'Lady, she liked the sound of shopkeepers on the telephone saying, 'Yes Lady Charrington, certainly M'Lady.' Mrs Charrington seemed somehow – well, less *interesting*.

'Well, now, up we get,' said Lord Charrington. He ran his hands through his thick grey hair so that his bald patch became covered and jumped out of bed. He was a big, thudding man, and the fact that he was about to turn into Mr Charrington had filled him even fuller of energy than usual. 'We have a great deal to do. Come on, darling. Come on, Jane. You must go and sort out your toys. Just remember, though, a council house is very small.' And again he made a small square in the air, as though they were going to live in a matchbox.

The next week was extremely busy. Jane went carefully through all her possessions and decided that she really needed them all. Lady Charrington not only went through her possessions but through much of the Castle and came to the same conclusion. Jane would pass her in the corridors, her tall thin frame looking rather odd on a vacuum cleaner, with one of the under butlers running beside her with a list, while she said, 'and *that*, and *that*, and *that*, and *that*.' Lord Charrington, although he had said they could all take what they wanted, at first tried to make them take a little less. 'Remember, darling,' he said, 'we shall only have four rooms in our new house.' But in the end, partly because he was himself finding it very difficult not to take things like all his guns and all his fishing rods, he let them do as they wanted. He said that perhaps they should learn gradually how to be Mr and Mrs and not in one jump. He began to talk vaguely about buying two or even three council houses.

But the most important reason for his not minding was that he was still in a great state of excitement about becoming Mr Charrington. He put several announcements in *The Times* and in all the local papers; he had ten thousand sheets of new writing paper printed with *Mr Christopher Charrington* at the top; and he went round telling everybody to call him Mr Charrington now and even Christopher or Chris if they liked, although the papers in London had not yet been signed.

Lady Charrington took quite the opposite point of view. 'I shall call myself Lady Charrington until the last possible *minute*,' she said.

The result of all their searches was that a continual stream of servants poured from the Castle carrying chairs, tables, pictures, books, carpets, curtains and everything else one can imagine. And a fleet of enormous furniture vans soon stretched all the way from the front door to the Lodge.

Jane enjoyed all this very much. She didn't mind what her parents were called: Lord and Lady Charrington, Mr and Mrs Charrington, or even Mr and Mrs Sausage. What she did mind was that somehow she must get the Book packed away and taken to their new house.

Her chance came the night before they were to leave. Lord Charrington had decided to speak to all the servants in one of the Great Halls. He had arranged that when they left all the servants would be taken on by the various organizations which were to move in. All, that is, except Mrs Deal. She was to accompany the Charringtons into their new council houses. But he wanted to tell them this. He also wanted to thank them all, since many of them had worked for the Charrington family all their lives; he wanted to speak about his new life, about the new England and why it didn't need titles, and also, for the hundredth time, explain how he had decided to be like them, a plain mister.

Jane found that she was sitting at the back of the hall next to her friend Simon. After her father had been speaking for a little while, she leant forward and whispered in Simon's ear. 'Follow me,' and quietly slipped out into the passage.

In a moment, Simon had joined her. 'What is it then?' he whispered.

'I'll tell you in a minute,' Jane whispered back, 'but we've got to hurry.' She ran to the store room and fetched a long coil of rope which she had seen there that afternoon, also a torch, and then went and collected two vacuum cleaners.

It took Jane a little while to persuade Simon that the old library wasn't haunted, but eventually, ashamed of seeming a coward in front of a girl, he agreed to go in. Once inside, they tied the rope firmly round the Book, passed the rest of it through a large ring in the library door and tied it fast. Lastly they tried to get the Book through the window.

It was extremely heavy, but by resting it on a chair and then both heaving at once they managed to get it first onto the sill and then sent it toppling out. At once the rope tightened and they heard the Book bumping against the outside wall of the tower.

Now they slowly lowered it hand over hand, until, when the rope went suddenly slack, they knew the Book had landed.

Immediately they hurried out of the library, onto their cleaners and roared back again. Ten minutes later they had carried the Book to the Land-Rover in which Jane and her parents were to travel, hidden it under some rugs, and were sitting in the back of the hall in time to hear Lord Charrington cry –

'. . . and so, from this moment on, I want all of you to put Lord Charrington from your minds. Let me be plain Mister Charrington. Mr Christopher Charrington, an ordinary scientist, like yourselves.' After a few embarrassed cheers and some hand-clapping, the hall emptied. Jane was sent early to bed as they were to start next morning at six o'clock.

The day dawned fine and sunny. From the start, all was hustle and confusion, with forgotten things being re-membered and Jane's mother wandering about as though in a dream. But all too soon, it seemed, they were ready to go.

Mrs Deal, who was crying, had been comforted with a little gin and put into the back of the Land-Rover warmly wrapped in rugs, among piles of luggage. Lord and Lady Charrington, or rather Mr Charrington and Lady Charrington, and Jane climbed into the front. There were waves from the servants gathered at the windows and then they were off.

A little way down the drive, where it rose over a lump, Lady Charrington said, 'Stop a moment, Christopher, let's just look back.'

Lord Charrington stopped the car and they all looked.

Curl Castle rose huge, magnificent and beautiful in the golden early sun. Its windows flashed, the creepers waved upon its high walls. There was the long roof where Jane and Mrs Deal had sheltered from the waters when the dam burst. There were the windows to the nursery and Jane's bedroom. Rising high to the left of the castle was the observatory. Far to the right, the tower of the old library, where so many adventures had begun and ended. And round about were the woods and fields where Jane had played so often.

And all at once Jane felt very sad. This had been her

home. Only now did she properly realize that they were leaving it for ever. In a small voice, she said, 'Daddy, we can go back sometimes, can't we?'

'Of course, said her father, 'of course. But naturally on visiting days. And then we'll be like ordinary people. We'll pay our 10p like everyone else. Unless, of course, we go to the Mental Hospital, in which case we'll have to prove that we are mad.'

But Jane's mother put her arm round her daughter's shoulders and kissed her. 'You can go back whenever you like, darling,' she said, 'you can spend all your holidays there and as much time as you like. We may well take a flat there.' She kissed her again and Jane kissed her back. At the same time she slipped her hand under a rug near her in the back. Beneath it she felt the hard, comforting corner of the Book.

'And I've got you, Book,' she whispered to herself. 'I can go to you whenever I like.'

'Ready?' called Lord Charrington, 'well, off we go then.' With a loud poop of the horn, the Land-Rover shot forward, and in a few moments Curl Castle had disappeared behind them, hidden by a clump of trees.

FICTION

Monica Dickens

FOLLYFOOT	20p
DORA AT FOLLYFOOT	20p
THE HOUSE AT WORLD'S END (illus)	20p
SUMMER AT WORLD'S END (illus)	20p

Honor Arundel

THE HIGH HOUSE (illus)	20p
EMMA'S ISLAND (illus)	20p

Glyn Jones

THE DOUBLEDECKERS (illus)	25p

John Montgomery

FOXY (illus)	20p
MY FRIEND FOXY (illus)	20p
FOXY AND THE BADGERS (illus)	20p

TRUE ADVENTURES

Richard Garrett

HOAXES AND SWINDLES (illus)	20p
TRUE TALES OF DETECTION (illus)	20p

John Gilbert

PIRATES AND BUCCANEERS (illus)	20p

Aidan Chambers

HAUNTED HOUSES (illus)	20p

NON-FICTION

These and other PICCOLO Books are obtainable from all booksellers and newsagents. If you have any difficulty please send purchase price plus 7p postage to PO Box 11, Falmouth, Cornwall.

While every effort is made to keep prices low it is sometimes necessary to increase prices at short notice. PAN Books reserve the right to show new retail prices on covers which may differ from those advertised in the text or elsewhere.